PANTO GIRL

A Romantic Comedy With No Boundaries

KERRIE NOOR

PANTO GIRL

Diva Diaries Book 3

JUST A THOUGHT

Panto is the king of satire
But only for those who speak English

CONTENTS

Glossary   7

1. The Blogger   9
2. The Bus Trip   13
3. Lochleekie Caravan Park   17
4. Nellie the Elephant   22
5. The Tea Break   28
6. A Kettle of Fish   33
7. Saving the World   38
8. Fags and Wind Machines   42
9. The Retreat   46
10. The Pole Dancer   50
11. Hens and Things   55
12. Fags   60
13. Stopping Traffic   63
14. The Dressing-Down   69
15. The Laundry Room   74
16. Morons   78
17. Lucinda   81

Epilogue   87
Lockdown   91
A note from The Author   97
Also by Kerrie Noor   99

GLOSSARY

"A different kettle of fish": The British equivalent of the American "a whole new ball game."

Braw: The Scottish term for "great!" Can be accompanied by "braw," "bricht," "moonlicht nicht," or "the nicht," which are impossible to say without a Scottish accent.

Hen: The Scottish slang for women. Originated from the time when every house had hens—and men, having difficulty remembering more than one name, called all females "hen." The same does not apply to men and cockerels.

"Lead in his pencil": Nothing to do with pencils and everything to do with a man's ability to *rise to the occasion*. The saying originated in the good old-fashioned days before the ballpoint pen and Viagra, when a dram was reputed to "put lead in your pencil" (the truth being get the woman drunk and her memory of the pencil, leaded or not, is completely blurred).

Greeting: A Scottish word for crying, i.e., "greeting features," "greeting face," and "shut your greeting hole," not to mention "greeting bairns" —Scottish for "baby," "child," "toddler," or something small that needs escorting to the toilet. (No crying, however, is implicated when used in the term "greeting card.")

Bawling: The same as "greeting" but much uglier, involving a runny nose, toilet paper, and probably some dribbling.

Spew: Aussie slang for vomiting, banned by mothers who want their children to sound educated or at least get a job.

Banter: Scottish for witty repartee usually spoken in the sort of Glaswegian accent that only the Glaswegian can enjoy, laugh about, or partake of.

Kipping: Nothing to do with Kipling cakes and everything to do with a nap that is too short for snoring but long enough to wake confused.

Chapter One

THE BLOGGER

The Meeting of Minds Under the Lubrication of Beer Is Often More of a Collision.

Helmut, a blogger of German origin, had just sat through a two-hour open mic session at the Stand and he hadn't laughed once. Helmut found the session as painful as a G-string two sizes too small; he was confused. He had always prided himself on his keen sense of timing and dry wit, and yet he left unmoved.

Helmut spent his time traveling while blogging about anything alternative, organic, and hopeful, and he had a good following. He had this idea for a piece on laughter therapy and decided to start with the great British dry wit.

Now he was confused . . .

Helmut walked down Great Western Road, pondering the use or abuse of the English language by its natives.

He had researched his subject before he left Germany and the Stand was *the* comedy club in Glasgow, where all the best comedians performed.

Perhaps Tuesday is not the best night to visit.

He spied a pub advertising German beer and went in. It was the same pub Lesley liked to visit, and as she was the only person sitting at the bar, he pulled up a stool beside her and offered her a drink. When she said "Maisel's Weisse," he looked at her with more interest.

Lesley had a fondness for German beer, and as they worked their way through the selection, Lesley began to open up. By the time Helmut was on his third pint, Lesley's accent became easier to understand . . .

"It was the teapot outfit that did it," said Lesley. "I told her if she was going to wear that onstage, I would not be responsible for my actions."

"Your partner is wearing a teapot?" said Helmut. "This is funny?"

"Nothing's funny about my ex," said Lesley. "Especially her principal boy."

"Principle boy?" said Helmut.

"About as camp as steak pie," she said.

"Begging your pardon?" said Helmut. "Principle boy?"

"Aye, you know, a woman dressed as a man . . . dancing . . . singing?" said Lesley.

"This is funny?" said Helmut.

"About as funny as herpes," said Lesley.

Helmut smiled. He knew about herpes.

Helmut was a young man with an earnest face and long legs that got in the way of everything. He was an ex-media student with parents who knew everything, including the great "tartan colony" of Scotland. Helmut had grown up on tales of bagpipes, football hooligans, castles, and shortbread: nothing like the Great Western Road he had just walked down. It was full of people from other countries. In fact, he was served by an Australian, got in the way of a Serbian cleaner, and managed to trip up an Indian—all in the one pub.

Lesley was the first real Scot he'd talked to, and he had lots of questions to ask. However, all she wanted to do was talk about the "frigging Pantomime," her "ex" and how "glad" she was to be "rid of her," and how "all the gay bars are best avoided," and she was not easily diverted.

She, having just left her partner along with all "her pantomime rubbish," had months of bottled-up emotion, and three pints down, Lesley was simmering with sarcasm as she launched into her descriptive criticism of the Riding Room, a three-point-nine-star gay bar.

Helmut interrupted her. "I am not gay," he muttered.

"That, my friend, is obvious," said Lesley with a tilt of her pint.

Helmut, unsure how to take such a comment, ordered another beer.

After their fourth pint, Lesley and Helmut moved to a table, where his legs sprawled out in front him tripping up the odd drunk.

Lesley pulled out the Stand leaflet poking from Helmut's top pocket and after a quick flick said, "That's your problem."

"Begging your pardon?" said Helmut.

"Tuesday is Red Raw night, or as they laughingly put it here, 'a night of new talent yet to be discovered.'" She drained her pint. "Heard that before." She tossed the leaflet across the bar. "The clue is in the '*raw*' so-called talent."

Helmut, with a downcast look, folded up his leaflet. "It is all, as you say, becoming clear," he muttered.

"That's what they said at the panto players," said Lesley, "'make way for new talent.' Sent my ex loopy trying to beat the new talent. And for what? To prance about a stage in thigh-high boots?"

"I have given up on the comedy," he said, trying not to think too much of thigh-high boots.

"You should have tried Friday," said Lesley.

"Maybe skip the clubs," muttered Helmut.

"Mind you still a hit-or-miss," said Lesley.

"I am really more interested in healing than stage," he said.

"Should visit Lochgilphead then, that place could do with some therapy," said Lesley.

Helmut, a literal man, looked up Lochgilphead on his mobile. "And how do you spell this Loch-what?"

Lesley laughed, bemused. "I was joking."

Helmut, engrossed in his mobile Guide to Bonny Scotland app, didn't hear.

"I mean it's hardly worth the two-hour drive"—she looked at his app—"or the bus trip."

"Past Loch Lomond," Helmut muttered.

"On a bus?" she said. "Not exactly sightseeing."

He looked up. "Will there be bagpipes?"

"Bagpipes?" laughed Lesley. "On Loch Lomond? What do you think they are, wild animals?"

Helmut, thanks to a few pints, was now in sync with Lesley's barbed comments. He threw his head back and let out a hyena-like laugh that stopped the pub.

"Jesus," muttered Lesley.

Helmut loved to laugh, especially at things no one else saw funny. A date for Helmut usually ended at the first joke.

He stared down at his app. "I come from a small village. It too is full of funny people."

Lesley eyed him suspiciously and sipped her pint. "There is Deirdre's creams, I suppose." She looked at Helmut.

"Creams?"

"Yes, she sells them in her Vegan is the New Black shop."

"Black? Vegan?"

"And Daisy's salon."

"Daisy? Is this not a flower?"

"She does a spot of massage, although I hate to say not on a par with Deirdre's." Lesley wiped her mouth.

"Then why say this?" said Helmut.

Lesley pushed her empty glass towards Helmut. "Funny man, aren't you?"

"You, Lesley, are the first to say this—where I come from, they say *seltsam*."

"What's that mean?"

"Weird."

Chapter Two

THE BUS TRIP

One Man's Pun Is Another Man's Gripe.

elmut knew a good story when he heard one, and he decided to head up to Lochgil-*whatever-you-call-it* and nose around. With a keen eye on his carbon footprint and no driver's license, Helmut caught the bus. Helmut was last in the queue, and the only seat left was in the front next to Madge, a large granny-like woman with a day's shopping piled on the spare seat.

With a grunt and glare, she emptied the seat and returned to her mobile, ignoring Helmut's thank-you.

The bus was full of people who seemed to know not only each other but also the bus driver—a phenomenon not new to Helmut, who had grown up in a small town himself. The only thing new to Helmut was the accent and the strange things that tickled the funny bone of a Scot, which to Helmut it seemed was *anything*. And yet that same *anything* could also elicit a spark of abuse, a stream of swear words, or worse, words used in a way his English teacher never taught him.

He spent most of his journey suppressing his emotions, especially his laugh, which left him with a weird lopsided smirk that most found, as he put it, *seltsam*.

In front of Helmut and behind the driver sat Pete, who appeared to be on best-buddy shouting terms with the bus driver—who, despite his hearing aid, seemed to need everything repeated at least once.

The great panto fire was in the local paper and what pretty much everyone was talking about, including Pete and the bus driver . . .

"It was George who started it," said Pete, tugging at his crisp packet.

"What?" said the bus driver.

"George!" shouted Peter. "He started the fire."

"That knob-head," muttered the bus driver.

"He lit a chimenea," shouted Pete as his crisp bag burst open, scatting crisps onto the floor. "Bugger."

"Chimenea? On a stage!" shouted the bus driver at the windscreen. "Where's the extraction fan? You need an extraction fan."

He shook his head, steering the bus around a roundabout.

"Can't have a fire without an extractor fan—not inside, health and safety. Everyone knows that."

"Well, he didn't," said Pete, sliding what was left of his crisps into his mouth.

"And that hall's not new, it's old, go up like a friggin' firelighter," said the bus driver.

"Used a packet of them as well," said Pete with a slight spray of crisps.

"What?" The bus pulled up behind a cyclist flying around the road. "Jesus!"

"I said he used a packet of fire lighters!" said Pete. He tutted. "You've your hearing aid on?"

"I heard he used a packet of firelighters," shouted the bus driver. He shook his head. "Mental . . . as mental as this friggin' cyclist." He opened his window. "Get off the road!"

The cyclist swerved around a corner.

The bus stopped at a traffic light, and Pete leaned nearer to the driver. "Your hearing aid switched on?"

"Nah, too noisy."

"So, what are you wearing it for?" Pete said.

"Health and safety," said the bus driver.

Pete sat back. "Christ almighty."

"What about the smoke alarm?" shouted the bus driver.

"What about it?" said Pete.

"Must have gone mental," said the bus driver.

"He switched them off," said Madge.

Helmut looked at her.

"Switched the alarm off?" The bus driver blew threw his teeth. "Christ almighty."

"Now he hears," muttered Pete.

A teenager approached the driver with a bored face. The driver pulled into the bus stop and turned to Madge. "Who'd do a thing like that? No one sane I tell you."

The bus pulled away . . .

"Switching the alarms off, for a pantomime." The bus driver shook his head. "That man's a pantomime I'll tell you . . ."

Helmut looked at the plump profile of Madge. She had spent most of the journey engrossed in Facebook.

"Chimenea?" Helmut muttered.

"Aye, you know, an *ootside* chimney." She looked back at her Facebook.

"Aren't they all," Helmut said with a glint in his eye, "*ootside?*"

She eyed him. "Funny man."

"Yes, but this is portable," shouted the bus driver.

Pete looked from Helmut to the bus driver. "How come you hear him?"

"A portable fire?" said Helmut.

"Sort of like a barbecue," sighed Madge, still engrossed in her Facebook.

"But with wood," shouted the bus driver.

"You have barbecues in Scotland?" said Helmut.

Madge threw him a look. "Yes," she said, "we are quite civilised you know."

Pete turned to Helmut. "Where you from, the North Pole?"

"Germany," said Helmut with a lopsided smile.

"That George has always been funny," shouted the bus driver. "Have you seen his caravan site? It's the place where caravans go to die." He chuckled at his wit. "In Lochgilphead, a town where folk go to die."

"I'm from Lochgilphead," said Madge.

"Me too," said Pete.

"He was on the stage you know," said the bus driver.

"George was on the stage?" said Madge.

"I heard he was in the army," said Pete.

"Yes, *on* the stage *in* the army," yelled the bus driver.

"Jesus, only asked," muttered Pete.

"No friggin' common sense," muttered the bus driver.

"What?" said Madge.

"I said that's stage folk for you, no common sense," shouted the bus driver.

Helmut was about to ask *what stage folk*, but catching Madge's eye he decided not to; instead, he flicked on his cheap rooms app and searched Lochgilphead.

Madge peered over his shoulder, took in Helmut's student/travellers-type outfit, and said, "You should stay at the caravan park, it's dirt cheap."

"Don't listen to her, it's a scrapyard," said the bus driver.

Helmut looked up Lochleekie Caravan Park on TripAdvisor. It had one zero-star review.

"*Dump* is too kind a word for that place."

"Do they have a chimera there?" said Helmut, thinking he was funny.

"Hardly, you're lucky if the showers are working," shouted the bus driver.

Chapter Three

LOCHLEEKIE CARAVAN PARK

Life Is Too Short for Nescafe.

Helmut arrived in Lochgilphead on a Saturday at lunchtime. He walked into the caravan park and straight to the shedlike reception and stared at the *George Pumpernickel Esquire* inscribed in gold across the entrance.

The door hung limply from its hinges; one kick would have dislodged it. Helmut, a polite man, didn't touch the door but rather shouted several times and then knocked on the wall. The door creaked open and two hens trotted out. Helmut, a man not comfortable with hens, decided to take a stroll.

He passed several caravans, most in need of some "TLC," as his English teacher liked to say. Finally, he stopped at a poky caravan the size of a matchbox with a weird-looking pink taffeta apparition hanging in the window.

More to this place than outside chimneys, he thought and took a photo.

"Can I help you?" said a gentle voice from behind.

Helmut turned around to see Charlie's kind face.

"I am looking for a caravan," said Helmut.

"Seriously?" said Charlie.

"Yes," said Helmut.

Charlie eyed Helmut. "You want to stay here?"

"Of course," said Helmut.

Charlie with a confused look took Helmut back to the reception. Helmut again looked at the *George Pumpernickel Esquire*, this time pondering a joke about bread.

Charlie interrupted his thoughts ("Crazy name, huh?") and motioned Helmut in.

The office was small and damp, with old pictures on the wall of a round man at various stages of baldness dressed in jodhpurs and boots like a director from the 1930s. Helmut stared at a picture of George, a megaphone in one hand and an arm around an actor in a green and purple wedding dress with a forced thumbs-up smile.

"His first panto," said Charlie.

"Looks like fun," said Helmut.

"Fun, with George?" Charlie pointed to the wedding dress in the photo. "See that dress?"

"Hmm, a prominent costume," said Helmut.

"We have lost more performers to that dress than sold raffles tickets."

"It is a hideous dress," said Helmut.

"That man there left the stage—for good. Took up book binding," said Charlie.

"Interesting," muttered Helmut.

Charlie handed Helmut a key, pointed to a caravan with a view of the loch, and then, with an "I can't believe you are staying here" look, broke into a spiel about the laundry hours and the secret whereabouts of the laundry key.

"I'm off to a meeting, but you can get me on my mobile." Charlie smiled. "If you need anything that is."

"I am alone at this park?" said Helmut.

"No," said Charlie. "You're the second to arrive and there's more booked. No idea why. Worked my socks off getting the caravans ready."

Helmut watched Charlie head for his meeting, then pushed the caravan door open and stared at the seventies interior: fake wood-panel walls, a two-ring gas stove with a box of matches perched beside it, and a strong whiff of bleach.

He ran his fingers along a surface: *spotless*.

He huffed his backpack onto the table, flicked the lights on and off, open and shut the fridge, then flopped on the bed. His phone pinged. He looked at it: more reviews of the caravan park, each wittier than the other . . .

Some even had Helmut laughing.

Helmut sensed he was on an adventure, something bigger than he first thought.

He felt excited.

Helmut loved his work; sometimes he felt the luckiest man alive. The only thing missing was someone to share it with, a girl with the same sense of humour, who *didn't run a mile when he laughed.*

He pulled out his portable coffee cafeteria and his organic fair-trade ground coffee, boiled the kettle, and stared out the window. In distance, on the green, Helmut saw a pin-sized Charlie surrounded by people and barking dogs.

Funny place to have a meeting, thought Helmut, *seltsam.*

After a coffee and a decent amount of time staring at the ceiling over his bed, Helmut decided to head for the Vegan is the New Black shop.

Charlie's meeting on the green didn't last long. In fact, Helmut was still sipping his coffee when the group left en masse.

Helmut slipped his iPhone into his pocket and headed out the door. Shooing hens from the steps he skidded, yelped and landed on a muddy patch while the hens squawked and fluttered about him.

As he lay by the steps, he heard the words "mutiny" and stopped . . .

A hen pecked at his feet, another his hands.

"Shooo . . ." he hissed.

The voices sounded closer . . .

"Surprised about that Derek," said a man's voice, "never thought he had it in him."

A hen pecked at Helmut's ear and with a swift automatic flick Helmut had the hen squawking like it had been kicked.

"Who's that?" shouted the man's voice.

Helmut sat up and stared into three faces.

The freckled face of a red-haired postman, Heather—also red-haired, but dyed—and a thin young woman with an earnest look and blond hair who Heather called Red.

It was Red who caught Helmut's eye.

Red, a single mother, had been asked to play Red Riding Hood in the pantomime by three successive directors, Derek being the last. It was her first pantomime, and she happily embraced the name Red due to hating her own given name: Glenderella. A name that was annoying, so old fashioned no one had heard of it, and the butt of her ex's jokes.

The most she had hoped for was a shortening to Glen, which usually led to such comments as "Are you gay?"; "I thought you were a boy"; and "You sure you're not gay?" Of course, being thin and built like a teenage male gymnast didn't help; neither did working in her father's garage spending most of her time greased up in overalls under a car bonnet.

Red had been a single mother since "her two" started nursery, and now approaching forty, she wanted to branch out, do more than "taxi her two" and remind them there was more to life than mobiles and saving the planet.

"Red," as she'd told her two unimpressed teenagers, "is a new name for a new beginning." And she had plans for more changes.

"Jesus, Mum, can you not just get your eyebrows waxed like other women?" said Kim, her daughter.

Red had told her daughter not to "talk like that," which in the end led to more talking "like that."

Her son Toby had said nothing. What was the point? His mother was a philistine.

Red looked down at the lanky student-looking man and assumed it was poverty that had him staying in such a rundown place. "Are you alright, hen?" she said in a warm voice.

Helmut stopped. "The hens? They've gone?" He looked around hopefully. "Haven't they?"

The three laughed. They seemed surprised to find anyone at the caravan park, and when Helmut told them he was not the only "camper," they laughed again.

"Camper?" said the postman. "Where you from, the brownies?"

Helmut, sensing a British pun, threw the postman a lopsided grin.

Heather looked about with a sniff, then pulled at a piece of metal hanging from the steps.

"It's a dump," she said. "Who'd stay here?"

"Charlie does," said the postman.

Heather flashed a look at the postman. "Apart from Charlie then?"

No one answered.

Helmut, brushing himself off, stood at attention and asked about the Vegan is the New Black shop.

"It's just a stone's throw away," said Red.

Helmut looked puzzled.

"We can walk you around," said Red. "Love that place."

"Me too," said Heather.

"Alright if you like tofu," muttered the postman.

"There is more to that shop than tofu," said Red. "Her creams work miracles, I mean look at Angus."

Helmut noticed a change in mood, and he was about to ask who this Agnus was when the postman spoke.

"They are trying to get her back."

"Shit, really?" said Heather.

Chapter Four

NELLIE THE ELEPHANT

Sex Has No Need for Comfort When Lust Is Involved.

When Helmut walked into the Vegan is the New Black shop, Deirdre, engrossed in creating an oil mix, didn't notice. She was preparing for a massage in the back room, and she was not happy.

The girls followed Helmut. Like most in the area, they loved the shop; there was usually something on sale and the smell was heaven. As they walked in, Helmut talked about his work, his interest in all things alternative, and how he wanted to change the world.

Red had no idea about such things—the only thing she knew about changing the world was the constant moans from her teenage son. It seemed everything she did was single-handedly destroying the rain forest, the planet, and his chances of making it through puberty, and she was about to say just that when Helmut caught her eye.

"I thought laughter was the answer," he said, "but it seems what makes one person laugh makes another angry . . ."

"Angry?" Red stuttered.

Deirdre appeared from the back storeroom grimly stirring.

"How's Agnus?" said Heather.

"The same," muttered Deirdre. She stopped and looked at Heather.

"I have tried everything from flower essence to Hawaiian massage, and apart from a good night's snoring, nothing has helped. I'm beginning to lose faith."

She returned to her mixing with increased vigour. "Maybe I can't massage after all."

Heather tried to reassure her as Deirdre made for a bottle of frankincense and knocked it off the counter.

Helmut caught it.

Deirdre stopped. "Oh . . . thanks."

"This is Helmut," said Red.

Helmut caught Red's eye, and for a moment time stood still as he thought he saw a soul as passionate about the rain forest as he was.

"You are having the heart of a vegan?" he muttered to Red.

Red blushed.

"And the rhythm for healing?" said Helmut.

Red laughed nervously. "Aye right, you should hear what my son says."

Helmut slid the bottle on the counter.

"Cheers," muttered Deirdre with a *he's weird* look at Heather. She dribbled a few drops of frankincense into her bowl.

"Frankincense, interesting," said Helmut.

"It's for calming the heart of a carnivore . . . of the worse kind," said Deirdre.

"Carnivore?" said Heather.

"Yes, but I can't say," said Deirdre. "It's hush-hush. All to do with the panto."

"Panto and massage?" said Red.

"Yes, and Lesley waits for no one."

Deirdre let out a frustrated sigh. "Bollocks, now look what you made me do."

"Lesley?" said Red.

"Lesley?" echoed Helmut.

"You're massaging Agnus's ex?" said Heather.

Deirdre nodded.

Heather blew through her teeth. "Shit."

"It seemed like a good idea at the time," muttered Deirdre.

"I met a Lesley in Glasgow," said Helmut. "She talked me through all the gay bars in Glasgow, until I told her"—he looked at Red—"I wasn't gay."

Helmut talked about his time in Glasgow and the Stand, until Deidre stopped him. "I can't mix and listen . . ."

"Tuesday was your mistake," said Red.

"Should've gone on a Friday," said Heather.

"Yes, this I have heard," muttered Helmut. "Still, this Lesley, she was helpful *and* funny."

Deirdre tutted. "Well *this* Lesley is as funny as herpes."

Helmut stopped. "Herpes?"

"Lesley's not one for laughing," Red said, flashing a smile at Helmut.

"She's more comfortable with a chainsaw," said Deirdre.

"She likes gardening," said Red.

"This Lesley never talked of gardening," said Helmut.

"Well it's not really gardening, it's more cutting things down, for a fire."

"A chimaera?" said Helmut.

"She'd laugh at chimaera?" said Deirdre. "Lesley's more a bonfire woman."

Helmut's face softened. "Massage can tame the heart of a lion, and with a few drops of ylang-ylang or jasmine, you might touch the inner Lesley"—he paused—"her goddess."

"Lesley's no goddess," said Heather. "She is a full-blown lumberjack."

"Hates all that womanly stuff. She'd rather tame a lion than be tamed," said Deirdre.

Red eyed Helmut's profile; it was quite delicious. She thought of a joke, then decided to change tact . . .

"You've any hair dye that's good for the environment?" said Deirdre.

Heather threw her a questioning look. "Environment?"

"Well yes . . ." said Red.

"Your son getting to you?" said Heather.

"Sort of," muttered Red, flashing a look at Helmut.

Helmut, now with a full-faced smile, gestured for her to go on.

Red talked of her new little Red Riding Hood role and how she wanted her hair to match.

Helmut eyed the gloss of her hair with an appreciative smile.

"Something," said Red, "that doesn't damage things . . . in the air, like . . ." Her voice trailed away as Heather glared at her.

"Damage things in the air?" said Heather.

"And . . ." stammered Red, "Deirdre is excellent at all things . . . organic."

"You on something?" muttered Heather.

Red shifted uncomfortably.

Deirdre looked from Helmut to Red. "You're never too old to go organic." She forced a laugh. "I mean if Lesley has agreed to a massage, anything is possible . . ."

Helmut spent a night in the caravan listening to lovemaking that had his imagination running wild. He had no idea the Scots could be so . . . adventurous, noisy, and, well, long lasting. He had heard they had no idea of foreplay, preferring the so-called "roll-on roll-off ferry method" his parents joked about.

His parents were as open as a barn door when it came to sex.

The British, according to them, had little interest in sex, preferring instead a laugh at something *dry* (whatever that was), watching TV in bed, and fish and chips (in or out of bed, he wasn't sure).

That night Helmut heard no TV, just "Nellie the Elephant" and *Thomas the Tank Engine* songs, along with odd giggling and a "once more into the breech, darling" shout. It went on for hours, the caravan rocking back and forth like a boat in a gale.

Deloris and Charlie's first night was the culmination of weeks of lusting, the great hall fire, and remarkably similar childhood memories (hence the nursery songs). Finally, they were alone by a wood-burning stove in a caravan the size of a pincushion.

Deloris had spent hours reliving the night of the great hall fire. The night Charlie picked her up, dropped her, and—with amazing recovery —not only picked her up again but saved her. She'd never been saved before. Her past exes thought remembering her takeaway order was heroic, doing her bra up was caring, and lust was a five-minute wonder spurred on by half a bottle of vodka. Charlie was different: he looked at her like she was a package with hidden secrets waiting to be explored and he was the explorer.

For the first time in his life, he felt like a hero, and this, to quote many a Scot, "put lead in his pencil."

Charlie, after years of enforced celibacy by his ex-wife, had forgotten how good it was to be touched, or for that matter where to touch a woman. Deloris wasn't short in telling him, and Charlie soon forgot about the German backpacker within earshot of their sighing, and the Australian couple Gary and Doreen on their gap year for pensioner's bike trip, a couple who had been together long enough to pay off several mortgages. Sex for them was something they switched off on the TV and, after a day's bike ride, was the last thing on their mind.

At dawn, Deloris, topless and with a glowing face, opened the caravan window, inhaled the morning air, and sighed.

"Thank God the park is empty," she chuckled.

Charlie, also topless but still in bed, started. "Bollocks, forgot about that."

"What?" said Deloris.

"There's been a few bookings," he said sheepishly.

"Shit," she said with an abrupt pulling of the blinds.

The same morning, Gary sat in the laundry block waiting on the drying of his smalls. He logged into his TripAdvisor app on his mobile and had just finished posting comments about Lochgilphead's "porno park" when Helmut appeared with a glazed expression . . .

With a fussy head from lack of sleep and an overactive imagination, Helmut took a seat and sipped his coffee. He thought "Nellie the Elephant" was a nursery rhyme, not a bonking song.

Gary began to empty a dryer. "No sleep, huh?"

Helmut shook his head.

Gary eyed Helmut. "Makes *The Last Tango in Paris* look like a pantomime, huh?"

Helmut smiled. His parents talked of *that* film.

"And I thought the Scots were as frosty as a bucket of ice."

Helmut smiled again. He had heard that too.

"Are you leaving?" said Helmut.

"Hardly, I'm taking notes," said Gary.

"Notes?" said Helmut.

"Too right," said Gary. He snapped the dryer shut and looked at Helmut. "Doreen was like a wild horse this morning."

"Wild horse?" said Helmut.

"Yes, turns out she had a thing for Nellie the Elephant." Gary rolled his boxers into a ball. "Twenty years of marriage and I had no idea."

"And Thomas the Tank Engine?" said Helmut.

Gary shook his head "Nah."

"I see," said Helmut sagely.

"But get this," said Gary, his face smooth and glowing. "Sex while trying to keep the noise down." He chuckled. "Amazing—it's like being a teenager again."

Gary shoved his rolled-up boxers into a basket and with a whistle spotted a coin on the floor. He looked at it, then with a "you need this more than me" smile handed it to Helmut.

Helmut stared down at the Queen's head, pondering the depth of humankind and sex as Gary headed back to his caravan.

The caravan door flew open.

"Coffee, extra froth?" said Doreen with a giggle.

"Super-large Cadbury Flake coming through," said Gary.

The door shut behind him as a final giggle filtered over the drum of the dryer.

Helmut twirled the coin between his fingers. For a moment he forgot about his blogs, his lack of sleep, and even the hen poop on his steps. Instead he thought about Red and wondered if she too was into froth, Flakes, and Nellie the Elephant.

Chapter Five

THE TEA BREAK

She Was a Buffet Rather Than a Dinner-for-Two Sort of Woman, Until She Met Her Soul Mate.

A few nights later, while Helmut was reworking his blog to match his radio piece, Red left for her first rehearsal with Derek, the new director.

Helmut was working on the idea of healing with erotic themes and nursery rhymes, while Red, her hair now organic red, was standing in the kitchen of the school mid panto rehearsal, pondering. She had been in that school many times thanks to her wayward children, but for once her pondering was not about her children.

Red had looked over her script a thousand times, memorising the words despite having a house full of teenagers. Red had perfected the art of switching off and could have memorised her lines in a hurricane. Schoolgirls "mucking about" in her daughter's bedroom could not put her off, nor a morose son stomping in and out of the kitchen.

She focused with a roll-up, a black coffee, and peripheral vision focused purely on her script. No matter how many times her son glared at her, she didn't see, and after half a dozen stomps, he could take no more.

"Must you suck on those cancer sticks?" he said.

"It keeps thousands of villagers in work," she muttered without looking up. She flicked a page and continued to lip-read.

The son huffed, pushed a glass under the tap, and turned it on in a temper. Water squirted onto his T-shirt.

Red, pretending nothing happened, flicked another page as her son, regaining his composure, left the kitchen accompanied by a loud slurp of water.

Red flicked on the kettle, idly wondering how tall that funny German in the Vegan is the New Black shop was. She tried to remember his name, then, giving up, wondered if her three-quarter-size bed was big enough for him and if he could be secretly installed in it without the son and daughter knowing.

She jiggled a teabag.

Fat chance.

She stopped, lost in the memories of the good ol' days shagging in the rain, a car . . . a caravan. What she wouldn't give for sex so good comfort was forgotten.

Heather, with a brisk entrance, took in Red's daydreaming and tea-making and huffed. "Derek wants to know when your father's coming."

Red, still jiggling, didn't hear.

"Something to do with the costume and padding," said Heather.

"Hmmm," sighed Red.

"And Derek's gagging for his tea," said Heather.

"The kettle's boiling," muttered Red.

Heather, pulling mugs from the cupboard, began to inspect the inside, blowing imaginary dust. "That postman is really getting on my tits," she said.

"He always gets on your tits. You should marry him," said Red.

Ignoring the marrying comment, Heather began dumping teabags into mugs.

"He's all fired up about special effects and has the sound girls at the point of walking off," snapped Heather.

"Walking off?" said Red.

"Yes," said Heather. "Honestly, that man is obsessed. 'Timing,' he says, 'timing . . . timing . . . timing . . .'"

Red watched as Heather rhythmically spooned sugar into each mug.

"He's like a broken record."

"Charlie doesn't take sugar," said Red.

Heather stopped. "Forgot about that."

"Neither does . . ." Red looked at Heather flustering over the mugs. "Forget it, I'll sort it."

"And he expects me to understand all this stuff," said Heather. "He's the one with a screwdriver. How am I to time a wind machine with the sound effects?" Heather opened the cupboard, inspecting the biscuit collection. "One minute I'm making coffee, buying custard creams"—she plonked a packet on the worktop—"the next budgeting funds. Now I am expected to deal with sound effects and a wind machine? I mean what happened to the good old-fashioned glockenspiel?"

Heather ripped at the packet of biscuits and the contents exploded onto the floor.

Red bent to the rescue. "They have a glockenspiel."

"And those girls don't listen to me," said Heather. She huffed. "They know best."

"They're schoolchildren," said Red, piling custard cream onto a plate, "what do you expect?"

"You'll need to speak to those girls, you're the youngest," said Heather.

"Youngest?" laughed Red. "I'm the mother of teenagers, not toddlers."

"Exactly, you're on their wavelength," said Heather.

"Wavelength?" said Red. "There is no wavelength with teenagers, just a constant stream of tuts."

"Yes, but you can interpret those tuts," said Heather.

Red tutted. She watched Heather make the tea.

"Derek likes his milky," she said.

Heather looked at her with a "please help" look.

"Oh alright," snapped Red. "But if the son finds out he'll kill me." She sighed. "Hates me talking to anyone remotely in his radar."

The postman was new to the area. He arrived the same day as a poster asking for volunteers to join the panto players went up in the co-op. He sauntered around to George's caravan park, took one look at the run-down reception, and offended George by offering to "fix things."

Unaware of any offence, the postman then offered to help with the pantomime.

"Any experience?" said George.

"Some," muttered the postman cryptically.

George, short on volunteers, agreed in his usual gruff manner, which went completely over the postman's head.

A week later, as George was surveying the community hall for the next panto, the postman was surveying the lighting system. As he sashayed down the ladder with a whistle, George asked him what his name was.

The postman, with a swing of screwdriver, didn't answer but rather tapped his nose, slid his screwdriver into his tool belt like a gun into a holster, and marched off still whistling.

The postman intrigued Red: he was an irreverent man of mystery, something short of in a town the size of a pea.

Lochgilphead was the sort of place where gossip echoed like a voice in a whispering gallery. Not an easy place to live when you had a daughter with a passion for underage drinking and fighting and a son intent on raising awareness of "all things green" via graffiti (his latest being "meat is a pile of puke" scribbled across the school canteen walls).

Her children were a trial that required a tough exterior, and the postman seemed the only person oblivious to her children's antics. He was more interested in getting the lighting right, especially for the much-talked-about pole dancing scene.

Heather, on the other hand, knew the postman purely on nodding terms until she joined the panto. Since then, the nodding terms had grown more into "I'll put up with you until the panto is over" terms.

She was a trim woman with tidy habits. She constantly tutted at his tools piled at the bottom of a ladder, paintbrushes left by unfinished scenes, and inability to provide any receipts for her books.

Receipts were everything, to her. "The foundation of a grant application," she called them.

The postman, it seemed, had as much interest in Heather's receipts as he did in Toby's "meat is a pile of puke" graffiti.

Heather worked for an accountant. She was a woman with a grown-up daughter in America and a solitary office job, all of which was a piece of cake when she came home to her delicious hubby; now there was no one to come home to, let alone cook for. Her husband died unexpected two years ago, and she still found herself turning to talk to him, rolling over to feel his body, and waiting for him to walk through the front door.

She never realised how lonely life could be, how shopping for one could drive one to drink and how "keeping herself busy" just made walking through her front door all the more depressing.

She dreaded the silence, sitting in front of the TV on her own, and, worse, waking up to herself. She, a no-nonsense woman of action, joined everything from the gym to the bowling club. She threw herself into charity work at the secondhand shop and of course the pantomime, but nothing helped. Everyone talked about their families, their partners, while she, wrestling with a head full of her own thoughts and no one to share them with, felt even more alone.

"Why don't you get a cat?" said her daughter one night on the phone.

"A cat?"

"Yes, then you have something to feed and pat."

But hubby hates cats, she almost said, and then with a tear she released it didn't matter what he hated anymore.

Chapter Six

A KETTLE OF FISH

Waxing—A Woman Feels Like a Woman When All Things Are Smooth.

While everyone was drinking their tea, Red headed over to Alisa and Ella posed by the sound desk. They were engrossed in their earphones.

Ella and Alisa were the same age as Kim, and nothing like her. They won awards for maths, did charity work, and were never seen loitering around the bus shelter.

The last time they caused any trouble was probably in their nappies, thought Red.

She sighed, attempting to catch one of the girls' eye, and when that didn't work, she knocked on the desk to get their attention.

In unison, they looked up with blank identical faces.

"You sisters?" said Red.

"No," they said in unison.

"It's just you look so alike . . ."

"Everyone says that," said Alisa.

"Not even cousins?" said Red.

"No," they said, again in unison.

Alisa slid her headphones back on as Ella eyed Red. "You're Toby's mum."

Red nodded.

Ella nudged Alisa. "Told you."

"Still a knob," muttered Alisa.

Ella huffed. She looked at Red. "I think he's amazing."

Alisa lifted off her earphones. "He's a dipstick. Anyone that writes 'meat's a pile of wank' on school property has no respect."

"It was 'puke,'" said Ella.

"Well, with that sort of gesture, 'wank' would have been better," said Alisa.

"It was an act of heroic proportion," said Ella, "and I for one salute him."

"You are only a vegan cause it keeps your stomach flat."

"That's not true." She looked at Red. "I love animals. I shop at the Body Shop."

Alisa tutted. "Where's your bag come from then?"

"Shut up," snapped Ella.

Red decided to change tack. "Heard about the wind machine."

Alisa slid her headphones off, placed them on the desk, and looked at her. "And what of it?"

"Well . . ." said Red.

"It's ridiculous," said Ella, "what they expect from us."

Red nodded.

"It's impossible," said Alisa.

Alisa gestured to the out-of-date sound desk, some of it held together with duct tape. "I mean look at this, it's as old as Super Mario."

"What?" said Red and Ella in unison.

Alisa waffled on about her cousin's vintage collection of video games.

Ella, clearly losing the will to live, muttered a "who cares," causing a look of venom from Alisa.

"What about the postman, is he no help?" said Red.

The two girls glared at the postman as he sauntered by with a whistle.

"Hey, girls," he said with a rhythmical swing of his screwdriver.

They watched as he made his way up the ladder.

"He thinks he knows everything," muttered Alisa.

"He so does," said Ella she gestured to the sound system. "Says any fool can work this crap."

Red nodded.

"And his wanting us to synchronise with that Lucinda, and she keeps changing things, and we're to change with her. Why can't she change to us?" said Alisa.

Ella, absently fumbling with a knob, said, "Shhh."

The postman flashed the lights on and off; the cast moaned.

"Sorry!" he shouted.

"Knob-end," said Alisa. "He always sticks up for her."

Red nodded. "It's the shorts."

"That what I keep telling her," said Ella.

"And the pole," added Red.

The next day, Helmut, uninspired, looked at his full list of therapists in the area. He wanted something different, juicy, and thought provoking. He wanted to create a blog that had his readers sitting up in their seats. He strolled past the Vegan is the New Black shop, idly wondering if that funny blonde called Red was there, and saw Deirdre packing towels into a bag.

She looked up as he waved and entered.

"You still here?" she said with disinterest.

"Yes, a curious town . . . and caravan park."

"So I've heard," muttered Deirdre, who like everyone else had heard of Charlie's night with Deloris.

"If you want something, you'll need to be quick," she said. "I have a massage."

"Oh?" He fingered a Buddha soap. "Lesley? Again?"

Deirdre lifted it from him. "You can always come back."

"Yes," he muttered as Red, spying Helmut, walked in.

Helmut admired her new bright red hair as Deirdre, with a harassed looked, eyed Red's casual entrance.

"If you want something, you need to hurry, I have a massage," said Deirdre.

"Lesley? Again?" said Red.

"Lesley waits for no one," said Deirdre with a frustrated sigh.

Helmut, oblivious to Deirdre's sigh, began to talk about taming the lion within.

Red listened and wondered . . .

Deidre interrupted him. "I am in a hurry . . ."

Red and Helmut looked at each other.

"I really must go," said Deirdre. She turned from Helmut to Red. "I'm running late."

"I see," muttered Helmut.

"Yes," said Red.

Deirdre pushed them out the door. She looked at the couple and softened. "Why don't you go for a coffee?"

Helmut and Red looked at each other across their coffees. Red nibbled on an empire biscuit, babbling to Helmut how they were "way better than a digestive." Helmut listened with fascination and, thinking he had a talent for reading people, brought two more. It was the longest Red had gone without a cigarette, and when Helmut launched into a monologue of jokes about his beer binge with Lesley, Red, giggling, forgot all about smoking.

"This Lesley was funny," said Helmut.

"She's a dyke," said an ol' fella sitting in the corner.

"Aye, but we're not talking about *that* Lesley," laughed Red.

"A woman that lives with a woman rather than a man is a dyke," said the ol' fella.

"Yes, but we are not talking about *her*," said Red.

"Especially when they get about like a joiner," said the ol' fella.

Helmut looked into Red's eyes. "Joiner?"

Red, with a "butt out of our conversation" glare at the ol' fella, explained that a joiner was a builder, and looking like one did not mean you were a dyke.

"The Lesley I met was also a dyke," said Helmut.

"Best not to say 'dyke,' 'lesbian' is preferable," said Red.

"You sure you're not talking about the same Lesley?" said the ol' fella.

Red, now ignoring the ol' fella, began to expand on the one-sided feud the sound desk girls held against the postman—or, as Helmut put it, "that nice red-haired man in a uniform"—and Lucinda.

"The girl with the long legs who rides a pole," said Helmut.

"Best not say 'ride' either," said Red. "'Dance' is preferable."

"Aye, 'ride' is a different kettle of fish all together," laughed the ol' fella.

Helmut stared at the toothless old man, quickly getting the gist of 'kettle of fish.'

"This kettle," he whispered to Red, "has nothing to do with boiling, has it?"

Red nodded.

Red relished a good audience and could tell a story with great animation. Helmut, with his soft Labrador eyes, listened on the edge of his seat, fixated on Red.

Red talked about Derek and how bad he was as a dame and how great he was as a director. "He is like a different person," said Red, "sort of grown up. He even looks taller."

"Yes, this is the phenomena known as confidence," said Helmut, waiting for another Red chuckle.

When she did, he sighed.

Chapter Seven

SAVING THE WORLD

A Man Will Hang on the Edge of His Seat to Listen to His Hero. A Women Does It for Her Man.

Helmut made himself at home in the caravan. He stared at the ceiling and thought of her sweet smile. He had spent a delicious afternoon with Red and not only walked her home from the coffee shop but ended up in her kitchen: the *Frieden de Widerstand* or (pièce de résistance).

He wanted her to feel his passion of all things green and healing, and as he talked of his passion, Red listened, finally laughing . . .

"When you talk of saving the world," said Red, "it sounds feasible; when Toby talks of it, it sounds like a childish dream."

"Toby?" said Helmut.

"Don't know where he gets it from, all this Greenpeace saving-the-world stuff," said Red.

"Who is *this?*" said Helmut.

"One day he's reading *Harry Potter*, the next Greenpeace," said Red. "Along with giving me lectures on paper bags and washing my cans out."

"Washing cans is a good start," said Helmut.

"Won't let me look at anything plastic," said Red.

"A knowledgeable man," said Helmut.

"His room is a hub of 'save the world' posters." She looked at Helmut. "For a thirteen-year-old, he takes my breath away."

"Thirteen?" said Helmut.

"Can't let him see it though," muttered Red.

"Toby is thirteen," said Helmut.

"Yes. Toby is my son," said Red.

"Arrr, the 'meat is a pile of puke' artist," muttered Helmut.

"Yes," said Red.

Red looked at Helmut; normally, this was the time a man made a hasty exit. Helmut, however, asked if he could meet this young man.

"Toby?" Red choked on her coffee. "You want to meet him?"

"Why yes, we all need a voice," said Helmut.

"You haven't met Toby," said Red.

"But I'd like to. An artist with cause—maybe I could put his thoughts in my blog," said Helmut.

A week later, Red appeared at her first rehearsal. It was a rehearsal heavy with suppressed emotion focused on anything but the panto.

Lesley, seduced by Deirdre's massages, had agreed to join the panto despite her ex Agnus also appearing in it. The first rehearsal was the first time they had seen each other since their separation. Lesley was having a fitting behind the curtains while the rest of the cast waited for Agnus to arrive, hoping a few sparks would fly.

Derek had his work cut out for him—focusing the cast was not easy. Derek, however, was a determined man, and he had the help of Charlie, who, thanks to Deirdre, was a new man with a much-talked-about "always the quiet ones" reputation.

Deirdre and Charlie had been together a week, and so far, according to gossip, they were hardly sleeping, or "at it like rabbits," as the butcher liked to say.

People looked at Charlie with silent wonder: a man who could "go all night" keeping the infamous Deloris happy, a woman with a reputation for knowing the Kama Sutra backwards and forwards and tossing men aside like empty crisp packets.

Charlie arrived late, fresh from a caravan park busy with guests. The cast stopped, watching as he walked over with a preoccupied look, plonked himself next to Deloris, and slid his hands into hers.

"Don't know what's going on but the caravan park is full—again!" He looked at Deloris. "Worked my arse off getting things ready." Charlie sighed. "And that Gary; still there. Talks to me like I'm some sort of guru."

The postman, posed at the top of a ladder, snorted.

"Gary?" said Deloris.

"The Australian. Refuses to leave," said Charlie. "Says he and his missus are inspired."

"Inspired, that's a good word for it," muttered the postman.

"Their marriage regenerated," said Charlie.

"Must be the water," muttered the postman.

Deloris smiled to herself. "Wonder if all Australians are so . . . regenerable?"

The postman snorted again, and he was about to make a comment about reviews when Agnus entered the hall.

The cast stopped, waiting for Lesley's response . . .

When none came, the cast began to talk of "calling it a night," apart from the postman. He remained at the top of the ladder.

"Calling it a night" was not on his agenda.

He had spent the last few hours inspecting various sections of the ceiling, oblivious to getting in the way, the constant tutting, and the "must you" and "is that absolutely necessary now?" from Derek and Charlie.

After several "good lighting was never done in a day" comments from the postman, Derek and Charlie finally gave up and worked around the ladder set up in the middle of the hall.

As the cast began to trickle home, the postman, staring up into the void of darkness, sighed. *There was a lighting system up there somewhere,* he thought with a tuneful whistle. *If you could call it that . . .*

He shone a torch into the darkness. It was an archaic mess, and with such a short time frame . . .

He smiled to himself. The challenge inspired him.

Heather, with a tray full of empty mugs, passed by and tripped over a hammer.

With a loud crash, she tutted.

"Mind," he shouted.

"As if that's going to help," she snapped.

The postman peered down at her. "What's the long face for?"

"I can't lock up till you're gone"—she sighed—"and look at this mess . . ."

"They're still here," he said, gesturing to the sound desk.

"But they're packing up. Not like your chaos." She pushed the hammer with her toe.

"Great lighting doesn't come in a day you know." The postman grinned.

"So you keep saying," muttered Heather.

"And that Derek has plans, big plans . . . impossible . . . plans," said the postman.

Heather looked up at the postman. "Thought you were Mister Fix-It—a miracle man."

"Kind of you to say, but I have my limits," he said.

Heather huffed. "Don't expect me to help."

"Help," chuckled the postman. "You're pivotal, my main man. They're talking of wind machines and strobe lighting. I can't do it all, not on my own."

The postman slid down from his ladder and gestured to the sound effects girls packing up their equipment. "They haven't a clue. Think it's all about *glockenspiels* and penny whistles."

"Well, in my day it was," said Heather, not really knowing what she was talking about.

"Not now." He shook his head sagely. "We're competing with YouTube, iPhones, Sky—the audience wants something more than *Three Stooges* slapstick."

"What's Three Stooges?" said Ella.

Alisa threw her a look.

"Some call it comedy," muttered Heather.

Chapter Eight

FAGS AND WIND MACHINES

Why Buy a Cow When You Can Get Milk in Bottles and Different Flavours?

Red left the rehearsal early, tentatively appearing in the kitchen.

The house was silent.

Was he home yet?

She flicked the kettle on, looking for signs, his jacket, the fridge . . .

That night, she had dropped Toby off at the library for his first meeting with Helmut.

With a "let's see what this German knob has to say," Toby jumped out of the car, gave a tentative slam, and headed into the library, a place he haunted with requests for "saving the planet" books.

Red was desperate to find out how it all went. She poured herself a coffee, slid on the TV, and wondered: Was she doing the right thing?

She had met Helmut several times, and so had Toby. Toby liked Helmut and saw him as his friend as much as his mother's: a man wanting to save the planet, something his ignoramus mother knew nothing about.

And still, Helmut had no idea she smoked.

Red was attempting to give up before he found out and had cut her fags down to the odd incognito roll-up outside. Helmut was talking of a vegan picnic, and the last thing she wanted to do was light up a fag over a lentil salad. She wanted to hold hands over said salad, wake up to his lopsided smile, and tell a story in public just to hear *that* laugh stop traffic.

She began loitering outside her kitchen with a roll-up, screwing her fag butts into invisible balls for the bin. She tried to last a whole rehearsal without one, every now and then sneaking outside, sniffing her empty tobacco tin, picturing Helmut and his lentil salad, then heading back in.

She had met a man worth breathing fresh air for . . . and although they had done nothing but talk, she knew he would make her happy.

The easiest place not to smoke was at work; a smoke in a greasy hand was not something Red enjoyed. The hardest, however, was going without a smoke whilst learning her lines.

Kim, who was usually aware of little else except how she looked on Facebook, picked up the vibe the day she saw her mother slide an ashtray from Helmut's view.

"She doesn't smoke in front of him," she said to her pal Caroline, who with the nod of an expert muttered, "A dead giveaway."

Toby, however, also noticed his mother's change in smoking, and for the first time since his voice had broken, he encouraged her.

"Keep it up, Mum," he said whenever he saw her near an ashtray; he even offered to take her ashtrays to the charity shop.

That night after his meeting with Helmut, Toby swung into the kitchen even more enthusiastic about being a Greenpeace warrior. He slid his jacket onto the back of the chair, pecked a kiss on his mother's head, and went to his room without slamming the door.

Red's heart danced. She was definitely doing the right thing.

Heather's heart was doing anything but dancing. Derek and Charlie had managed to find a free wind machine and were hell-bent on using it. It was an opportunity too good to miss, especially in the presence of a pole dancer. And they wanted *her* to help the postman, claiming *she* was "pivotal."

Why me? Am I now a backstage hand as well as everything else?

She argued, but no one listened; instead, she was invited to the production meeting in the caravan park the next day. It was called a production meeting because the cast, meaning Agnus and Lesley, could be excluded.

The meeting was held in George the caravan park owner's lounge room. There was talk of George coming home from hospital, and Charlie had cleared the room. He had shifted piles of papers, paper coffee cups, and takeaway packets, leaving a room bare of anything apart from a couch with an imprint of George's body and dusty army memorabilia.

George, a morose man, was almost smiling at the changes Charlie had made to his caravan park (mainly that it was making some money), and he promised a thank-you surprise once "out of bed and back in action," as he put it.

Charlie wasn't holding his breath; George was the sort of man to forget things. He spent most of his time wheeling his wheelbarrow from one place to another, then forgetting what he was to fill it with, or, if filled, where he'd planned to dump said filling.

Charlie tossed a log on the fire and turned to the production team.

"We are here to discuss the chase scene," he said. He scanned the room. "Where's the postman?"

"God knows," muttered Heather.

"He's pivotal," said Derek.

"Pivotal?" said Ella, picking up a First World War tobacco tin. She blew the dust from it. "What's that when it's at home?"

"It means important, but even more important than important," said Alisa.

Derek, lifting the box from Ella, rubbed it clean and placed it back on the table, and he was just about to give his definition of *pivotal* when the postman's jaunty whistle filtered through the front door.

Accompanying his whistle with a jaunty swagger, he bounded into the lounge room and plonked himself by Heather on the couch. He had just delivered an adult toy to Gary, and he was not about to tell anybody; he loved the confidentiality of his job, unlike *some* of the morons in the sorting office.

Heather with a tut attempted a shift away, but the couch with its ageing cushion made shifting impossible. Each move she orchestrated plopped her nearer to the postman's thighs.

"Cosy," laughed the postman.

"Hardly," muttered Heather.

Charlie turned to the postman. "You want to explain about the wind machine to Heather?"

"If it has anything to do with that Lucinda and her pole dancing, I'd rather he didn't," snapped Heather.

"Same here," said Alisa.

Chapter Nine

THE RETREAT

Women—Why Buy an Entire Pig Just for a Sausage?

Helmut sat at the table in Red's kitchen. He and Toby had been for a walk.

It had been two weeks since they had first met in the library, and since then they had been on several walks. Helmut was a hit with both Toby and Red. Toby's morose face lit up at the mention of his kindred spirit, while Red looked forward to when Helmut and Toby returned and Helmut stayed for coffee. This time she had bought a few German beers, just in case.

Helmut watched Red spoon fair-trade coffee into her coffee maker. He was starting to feel at home in her kitchen. Over the visits he had brought a packet of empire biscuits, his dog-eared *Greenpeace: The Inside Story* for Toby, and a selection of organic vegan cheeses, which Red sniffed at before placing in the back of the fridge.

Helmut watched Toby retreat to his room. "I am thinking of a retreat for my next blog," he said.

Music blasted from Toby's room.

Kim barged through the back door, threw her usual "you're alien" look at Helmut, and made for the fridge.

Caroline followed with a "Hi, Red; *Hi*, Helmut."

"Retreat?" said Red. Her face lit up. "I've been on one of those."

Kim, ignoring Helmut, turned to Red. "Mum, you're not telling that stupid story again?"

"I think it's funny," said Caroline.

"Thank you, Caroline," said Red with a tilt of her can.

Kim stared into the fridge. "That story has no end."

"Story?" smiled Helmut.

"It goes on forever." Kim pulled several cans of diet *whatever* from the fridge.

"Forever?" said Helmut with a mocking look.

"You'll never get away"—she looked at Caroline—"and it's not funny."

"No story goes on forever," said Helmut.

"Hers does," said Kim, tugging Caroline to her bedroom.

Helmut looked at Red. "This I have to hear."

"No, you don't," shouted Kim, slamming her bedroom door, followed by shouting at Toby to turn his "rubbish music" off.

"Worth a beer?" he said, pulling a couple cans from his backpack.

Red flicked her can open, sipped, wiped her mouth and looked at Helmut.

"I won it in a raffle."

"Raffle?"

"You've been warned," shouted Kim.

"It was some sort of dance retreat, and the funny thing was there was no music . . ."

She emptied a packet of nuts into a bowl. Helmut slid a couple into his mouth.

". . . just rolling around on the floor with old men and hairy women," said Red.

"Rolling?" Helmut said.

"Not that I have anything against old men or hair. It's just that I don't like a mouthful of it, especially unaccompanied by music," said Red.

Helmut chuckled.

"The couple in charge were into all things tantric," said Red.

Helmut stopped, peanut suspended. "Tantric?" Their eyes met. "I know about tantric . . ."

"They spent their spare time in pursuit of the 'perfect massage'—in the lounge room—while we were still there," said Red.

Helmut coughed, a peanut stuck.

"They were like teenagers on Viagra," said Red.

Helmut let out a volley of coughs.

"It was enough to put you off your camomile," said Red.

Helmut gulped his beer. "Nobody likes camomile."

"They suggested we get in touch with our inner child . . ." Red stopped, beer hovering. "Or was it . . . animal?"

"Animal," shouted Kim, flicking on something loud.

". . . and make as much noise as possible," said Red.

Helmut nodded.

Toby turned up his music, Kim followed.

"We were given the 'freedom' to choose whatever animal we felt was lurking in the corners of . . . our inner whatever," said Red. "Cat seemed to be the most popular . . ."

Toby shouted from his room, "Mum, tell *greetin' features* to turn her music down."

". . . something to do with stroking and rubbing." Red warmed to her story.

"Stroking is good," said Helmut.

Toby barged into kitchen. "Mum . . ." He stopped. "Stroking? Who's stroking?"

"The animal inside us," said Helmut.

"She's telling the retreat story," shouted Kim over the end of a song.

Toby stopped. His mum only told that story to her dates . . .

"There was a man who carried his teeth in a Tupperware box, and a woman with a beard!" said Red.

Toby looked from one to the other; they hardly noticed him.

"Tell him about the sleeping," shouted Caroline.

"No, don't," muttered Toby.

"'I have this sleeping problem,' says the bearded lady. "'I drop off just like that . . .'" Red clicked her fingers. "'But don't worry if you find me snoozing on your shoulder, I never dribble.'"

Helmut let out another chuckle. He was in the presence of a great storyteller, one who would hopefully tell him more stories well into his old age.

"The elderly gent decided he was a gorilla—looking for a mate," said Red. "He stood up, beat his chest, and started to growl . . ."

"With or without the teeth?" said Helmut.

". . . and after his second coughing fit turned to a cat," said Red.

"Looking for a good stroke, I suspect," said Helmut.

Toby opened the fridge, shut it, then pulled an armful of bananas from the table. With a long face, he sighed. *Are they on a date?*

"That afternoon I tried to leave, but *they* stopped me at the gate," said Red. " "Don't be afraid of what you feel," they said, "this is your chance to heal—just be with it!"

"Salutations to the sun," smiled Helmut.

"Two days later I still had no idea what I was supposed to 'be with,' but I knew where I didn't want to be—at that retreat," said Red. "It was cleaning day and the last thing I felt like doing was polish the toilet after said gorilla."

Helmut let back his head and roared a full belly laugh that stopped the music in Kim's room. "What the hell was that, Mum?"

"Helmut's laugh," muttered Toby.

Red, laughing, pulled a beer from the fridge. "Oh, and everyone had a frigging cold!"

Helmut threw his head back and let rip.

"Another beer?" she said.

He could have kissed Red, and with the knowledge that in the future he would, he laughed. "Your secrets are safe with me."

Red gulped. She had no secrets, but at this point she wished she had.

"Secrets?" she said.

Helmut smiled cryptically.

Chapter Ten

THE POLE DANCER

Getting in Touch with the Goddess Within Requires No Hormones.

The postman and Heather worked hard on the chase scene. Together they had to work out the aim of the wind machine and time it with the sound effects, redesign a dilapidated Captain Hook boat into Grannie's soup kitchen, and design a beanstalk cover for the pole dancer's pole that not only looked like a beanstalk but had the ability to drop (to quote the postman) like a pair of knickers.

Everyone apart from Heather, Ella, and Alisa were eagerly waiting for the chase rehearsal; Lucinda's pole dancing was the climax. Lucinda was the principle boy, whose very name had most of the male cast weak at the knees. It was rumoured that she rehearsed in shorts tighter than a latex glove.

Ella and Alisa just wanted it all to be over. There had been so many changes to the sound effects that they had no idea what they were to do when, and they were sick of the sight of Lucinda prancing around.

Heather, fed up hearing about the "eighth world wonder," decided to see for herself what all this pole dancing was about and searched YouTube. Positioning herself with a coffee and oatcakes, she flicked through the many pole dancers, stopping at Freddie and his flamingo.

The flamingo intrigued her.

She flicked it on, slapped a cheese slice on her oatcake, and took a sip of coffee.

When she saw Freddie's flamingo, she, nearly choking on her coffee, forgot all about her oatcake. And when his flamingo took on a life of its own, Heather's cheese slice took a dive for the floor.

Heather watched as Freddie, in a G-string the size of a cupcake and a torso that screamed *lick me*, performed a floor dance on par with sex. By the time he was on the pole performing unimaginable things with his legs, Heather had tossed her coffee in the sink and opened a bottle of wine. Freddie deserved a full-bodied red, and a second if not third look.

She stared . . .

Is that humanly possible?

That night, Heather tossed and turned in her sleep as images of Freddie's smooth muscular thighs taunted her.

Her hubby was a man who had spent many hours making her happy. Freddie rekindled those memories, and she woke for the first time since his death with her pelvis throbbing with pleasure.

The next rehearsal, as she and the postman were trying a new calico cover-up beanstalk over Lucinda's pole, Heather's thoughts wandered to Freddie. Positioned at the bottom of the ladder, she tugged the calico tight as the postman at the top adjusted the wiring. Heather was unusually quiet. He looked at her; her blank face puzzled him . . .

"You think that calico is the way to go," he laughed.

Heather said nothing. Her silence threw him, and he fumbled with his screwdriver. "Just joshing . . ."

That usually got her going.

The postman waited for her to bite . . .

She sighed. "You ever seen pole dancing?"

Pole dancing? thought the postman. He looked down at her. "What did you say?"

"Pole dancing?" she shouted.

Ella and Alisa giggled.

The postman made his way down the ladder. "Pole dancing," he said, "is an art form."

"Art form?" said Heather.

"Much more than the maligned dance that many see," said the postman.

"Just asked have you seen it," said Heather. "Wasn't looking for a lecture."

"And way more than a romp of topless—" The postman stopped mid-sentence.

Lucinda appeared, inches from him. He inhaled her shampoo. *Vanilla?*

Lucinda looked up at the calico beanstalk with an impressed nod. "You do the impossible so well."

"It wasn't just him," muttered Heather.

The postman dropped his screwdriver.

Lucinda picked it up.

He blushed.

She smiled.

"We're just making a hole for your pole . . ." He stammered like a pubescent school boy.

Heather, a woman of many talents, had none when it came to tact, especially with the postman.

"What the hell are you talking about?" she said. "We don't need a hole at all, just a few drill bits and bit more calico . . ."

Ella and Alisa burst into laughter.

Lucinda looked at them. "What's so funny?"

The postman, wishing the earth would swallow him up, made his way back up the ladder.

Heather looked at Lucinda. *What's all the friggin' fuss about?*

Lucinda, unaware of Heather's *what's all the fuss about* look, turned to the sound effect girls.

"Why don't you cut that man some slack? He's only trying to do his best."

Heather, without a word, made her way to the kitchen. She had spent the last hour greasing the lever for the beanstalk drop, folding up said calico, and putting away the postman's tools, and did anyone help? Did anyone say "well done"? They were all too busy watching the sound effects girls get a telling off by Lucinda.

Finally, in desperation, Charlie took Lucinda backstage and shouted, "How about some coffee, Heather?"

"Me, make coffee?" said Heather

"Great idea," said a voice from the back.

"Be a luv," said the postman.

Heather huffed. She was fed up to the eyeballs. She joined the panto for fun, not to be a skivvy on all fronts . . . .

Now she was expected to make coffee . . . while Lucinda gets the VIP treatment. *Lucinda who never makes coffee . . .*

She headed into the kitchen to find a lovesick Red.

"I mean what am I, chopped parsley?" she snapped.

Red jolted. "Parsley?"

"I mean am I invisible?" snapped Heather.

"Hardly," laughed Red.

"Here I am knocking my socks off creating a soup kitchen out of a pirate ship, for what? So he can stand there and watch some young slip of a thing . . ." said Heather, she stopped, caught her breath, her chest heaved. "Just the mere mention of her name and he's gaga."

"They all are, it's the pole," said Red.

"Even the local dyke goes gooey-eyed over *her*," said Heather.

"I wouldn't call her that, she'll punch you," said Red.

"I mean what's so great about that Lucinda?" said Heather.

"I told you it's the pole . . ." Red stopped. "And the shorts."

"Yes, and that's another thing—why does she insist on wearing them to rehearsals?" snapped Heather. "It's winter, for Christ's sake."

"It just a panto, hardly worth . . ."

"A little acknowledgment wouldn't go astray," muttered Heather.

Red stopped and looked at Heather. "I think you're amazing," she said.

"After all, it was me who discovered the miracle of calico," said Heather. "*And* its ability to stand to attention . . ."

Red interrupted. "All those things you do . . ."

"What?" muttered Heather.

". . . and Dick Whittington," said Red.

"Oh, that?" said Heather.

"You stuck the un-stuckable," said Red.

"With superglue anyone could have done it," said Heather.

"The postman called it a resurrection," said Red.

"Resurrecting his Dick is what he said," said Heather, "couldn't help himself."

Red chuckled.

"Typical," muttered Heather. "Anything for a laugh."

"You made it into an excellent wolf," said Red. "That's what the postman said."

Heather looked at Red. "Did he?"

"Yes," said Red. "He'd 'never have thought of that,' that's what he said."

"Oh." Heather poured herself coffee.

Red pulled out the biscuit box and surveyed the collection. *Not a chocolate one in sight.* She huffed. "Typical."

Red thought about the night before. Helmut stayed on after the retreat story for tea and helped with the clearing up. She thought Toby would be happy. Instead he started stomping again.

Especially when Helmut kissed her goodbye. It was only a peck, nothing more, but Toby saw it . . . and said nothing. And when Toby said nothing, that was worse than something.

"Maybe you're a bit jealous," muttered Red.

Heather stopped. "Me? Of what? Why?" She paused . . . "No. Definitely not. Not me."

Red thought of Toby again. "Sometimes we're jealous and we are not even aware of it."

"Well, not me," stammered Heather. "I haven't a jealous bone in my body."

Chapter Eleven

HENS AND THINGS

Love Can Overcome Fear.

A few days later, George left the hospital. He arrived to find cars parked by caravans, machines whirling in the laundry block, and Helmut skidding down the steps of his caravan amidst a flutter of hens.

The hens had taken to parking themselves under his caravan away from the wind and rain.

Every time Helmut opened his door the hens appeared, clucking about his feet like there was something tasty beneath. He didn't feed them, but everyone else did, and by his caravan. They all wanted the eggs but not the mess, the clucking, or the soggy ground. The caravan steps were covered in hen poop and the ground about the steps was as slippery as oil. Stepping out of his caravan required the balance of an ice skater and the observation of an eagle.

There were perks: free-range eggs with orange yolks so fresh they were still warm, and happy hens—a sight to enjoy until one pecked, which, as Helmut reasoned, justified the taking of the odd egg to Red's house.

Toby disapprovingly sniffed at the misshaped eggs.

Since *the kiss* at the kitchen door—or *full-on snog*, as Toby called it— Toby's mood had dived, making Kim's ignoring of Helmut a breeze to deal with. Toby retreated to his room, refusing to meet his so-called soul mate, and took to stomping when Helmut appeared, especially when Red started baking cakes for Helmut with *said eggs* or he when started baking for her without. Toby even refused the much-talked-about vegan picnic.

Helmut pondered the complexities of a teenager . . .

From what he remembered, he spent his teenage years in his room avoiding sex and drug lectures from his parents. In truth, his open-minded, let's-lay-our-cards-on-the-table parents were the cause of introversion on a massive scale; they were way too liberal to be comfortable with. Their so-called lectures caused Helmut embarrassment on a par with standing naked at a train station . . .

A condom demonstration was not something you wanted to see from your mother, especially with your father maintaining *his* instrument was not a toy and putting on a condom was an art form and nothing like "pulling on a sock."

And as for their talks on drugs? They were more reminiscent of past adventures with spliffs the size of a frankfurter than a lecture.

Did anyone really want to hear all that?

He watched as George limped with purpose into his cottage. A hen flew up to Helmut's window, pecked the glass, and crashed to the ground with a squawk.

Helmut closed the curtain . . .

He could hear shouting and stopped to listen.

George was trying to get to grips with a caravan park full of campers and hens. "What the hell is going on?" he yelled.

There was silence . . .

The door slammed.

"But you just got here," yelled Charlie.

Helmut stopped. *George had arrived and was leaving again?*

Helmut had heard so much of George from Red. This was the director who had burnt down the hall to a rubble of bricks, who shouted through a megaphone, who not only had fought with the infamous Catrina but had lost?

"I am going to sort that witch out once and for all," shouted George.

Helmut was curious. He saw a blog or two—something interesting and juicy. He opened the curtain again.

George huffed into his car, revved the engine, and squealed an emergency James Bond reverse, startling the hens.

The car stalled.

"And that's another thing," he shouted, "these frigging hens; need to pen them in, this place is like a sewage plant."

George started up the car and, with a crunch of the gears, reversed into a hedge.

Charlie shouted something about "not driving" and his "leg."

George, however, was oblivious to Charlie. He heaved himself out of the car, slammed the door, and limped like a man possessed out of the caravan park.

Helmut had never seen anger like it, or a cane move so quickly. He marvelled at George. *Definitely a blog or three . . .*

Charlie gestured to Helmut, yelling something about the hens being at "sixes and sevens."

Helmut, wondering what "sixes and sevens" was, opened the window and shouted, "Pardon?"

He forgot about the hen . . .

The hen fluttered up.

Helmut, not quick enough to shut the window, squealed.

The hen, with a squawk, flapped onto the windowsill.

Her black eyes blinked at him.

Helmut froze . . .

Shit . . .

Helmut's discomfort of hens was on par with his discomfort for his parents' sex lectures, and a hen inside terrified him. All it took was one flap of a feather and Helmut's heart was beating against his rib cage like it was trying to escape.

Helmut gulped.

The hen clucked.

Why the Kronenbourg had he opened that window?

After three more *why the Kronenbourg*s, Charlie crashed through the door, sending the hen into nervous flapping.

She landed on the table.

The two men stopped.

They stared at the poop oozing from the hen's behind like ice cream from an ice cream dispenser.

"Shit," said Charlie. "What's she been eating?"

Helmut said nothing.

Charlie started to talk to the hen as she squawked, jumping from the table to the chair and then back onto the table.

"Come on, Jess," hushed Charlie, "there's a good girl . . ."

Poop oozed out of the hen like cream from a donut.

Jess began to coo.

Charlie manoeuvred himself behind her, herding her to the door.

"That's it, ol' girl, let's get you home . . ."

Jess, now clucking contently, trotted to the door.

"Good Jess," muttered Charlie, "nearly there."

Jess's claws tentatively stepped on the step . . . she was almost there . . . when . . .

Gary burst in like a bull on a rampage, scaring the hen into another frenzy of flapping.

Gary's caravan was on the other side of the hedge George had reversed into. And George had interrupted Gary and his wife . . . making coffee, so he said.

"What's up that George's arse?" he shouted, then stopped.

Hen poop was splattered everywhere like a Jackson Pollock painting.

Gary covered his nose. "Jess, mate, that stinks."

The hen landed on the table, skidded, righted herself, pooped, then trailed the poop across the table as she made for the window.

Gary made a lunge for her.

"Noooooo!" yelled Charlie.

The hen flapped like a wind flag in a gale.

Gary skidded and crashed to the floor.

The hen, seeing its chance, clambered over Gary's head and down his back, and with a squawk of freedom it flew into the air and fluttered out the door.

Helmut watched as Jess, embraced by her fellow hens, disappeared under a bush.

Gary stood up, brushed himself off, and stared at the carnage. "Maybe I should give the Indian takeaway a rest," he said.

Charlie stopped. "You feed my hens Indian takeaway?"

"Well . . . yes." Gary shifted uncomfortably. "But not the vindaloo . . ."

Chapter Twelve

FAGS

The Easiest Way to Break a Habit Is to Find a Better One.

George stomped to Catrina's and didn't return for several days. It was the talk of the caravan park, which now seemed more like a soap opera set, although no campers had yet met George. The only things they knew about him were the photos in the reception and his liaison with Catrina, an infamous woman who *took no prisoners*.

The Aussie couple regularly spent their mornings in the laundry, along with other campers. At first it was to talk about the antics of Charlie and Deloris, until George arrived.

George, a man old enough to collect a pension and lame enough to make it a disabled one, looked like the sort of man who struggled with a fumble, let alone to keep a woman like Catrina happy. And when he returned, everyone was desperate to hear the latest . . .

Soon George, unaware of his fame, was wheeling his wheelbarrow about, this time not in pink PJs but, thanks to Catrina, in wellies and mac.

The first thing George did was to move Charlie to a caravan out of earshot. One night of their lovemaking was enough for him. The second was to fence the hens in, along with a drake that had taken to following the hens about.

No one had any idea where exactly the drake had come from, but there were several rumours, one being that it was won in a raffle.

George, denying all raffle involvement, claimed the drake appeared one morning after he found a drunk farmer kipping under Charlie's old caravan—a story as plausible as George's rubbish fencing.

A few weeks later, the first act of the panto was in full rehearsal swing. Red, despite entertaining Helmut with stories of the rehearsal, was beginning to wonder if she was ever going to make it onstage. Lesley and Agnus held everything up with their constant fighting.

Red pulled a beer from the fridge and stared at her script. It had been a painful rehearsal. Agnus insisted on tap dancing when she was supposed to exit, sending the salsa team into a chorus of catcalling and the sound team useless with laugher, which in turn sent Lucinda into another lecture that had the sound effects girls pouting and Charlie calling for a coffee break.

She sighed. *How is the panto to get a laugh with those two bozos running amok?*

She slumped at the kitchen table as Toby walked in.

He stopped and looked at his mother staring at her script with what he thought was a look of longing for cigarettes. He, in one of his good moods, felt an urge to be a good son.

"Do you want me to help?" he said. "Read your script with you, take your mind off the fags?"

Red, choking on her beer, looked at him. "You want to help me?" she said.

"Yes, what's wrong with that?" said Toby.

"Well, nothing, I guess . . ." said Red. She quickly picked a scene.

Toby looked at the page and was just preparing to launch into his "all the better to see you" speech when Kim walked in.

She stopped. "What's going on?"

"He's helping me with my script," said Red.

Kim pulled a face. "Him, helping you?"

"What's wrong with that?" said Toby.

"Well, it's just that you never want to help anyone apart from friggin' Greenpeace," said Kim.

"She's trying to give up the fags," said Toby.

"Aye right," tutted Kim.

"So, I'm helping her," said Toby.

"By reading that?" said Kim.

Red nodded.

Kim paused at the fridge, opened it, then shut it . . . she looked at the two of them posed by the kitchen table.

Toby read a line. "All the better to see you with . . ."

Kim stared at him. "Really?"

"Yes," said Toby. "Being green is all about helping, and I am helping Mum."

Kim pulled the script from the table and looked at it.

"Here, let me," she said. "I'm way better at reading than him."

Red smiled with not one thought of a smoke. Instead she pictured Helmut, Kim, and Toby in the panto audience cheering her on.

Helmut had talked of many things, including manifestation: picturing what you want to make it happen. She hadn't even pictured this scene—her children helping her—and yet here they were. Her heart sang with the thought of a future together, and when Helmut walked in, she felt the picture was complete—complete bliss.

"You three reading the script—together?" Helmut smiled.

"Yes, we're helping Mum give up the fags," said Toby with a *you can bugger off* look.

Kim kicked him under the table.

"You smoke?" muttered Helmut with a disappointed look at Red.

Kim looked from her mother to Helmut. "Yes, but . . . she's given up."

"Trying to," said Toby.

Red said nothing. She saw the look on Helmut's face and could have strangled Toby if it wasn't for the fact that she loved him.

Chapter Thirteen

STOPPING TRAFFIC

To Catch a Hen Requires More Than Speed.

*I*t was the chase scene rehearsal everyone was waiting for, except for Heather. She was positioned on a beam close to the ceiling and looking down on the stage, feigning boredom. She had the beanstalk lever to push, and according to the postman, timing was crucial.

"It's all down to you," he said earnestly. "Lucinda's depending on it."

His words stuck . . .

Lucinda *the legs* was a love-or-hate sort of woman. Men loved her, and most women hated her. She had a strut that saw to that, a strut that rendered other women invisible, and with one flick, Heather could ruin it all.

The thought intoxicated her.

Heather peered down onto the hall. She could see the sound effects girls' heads bent over their glockenspiel, tinkering with boredom. Lesley and Agnus were walking through the chase scene, and *Miss Perfect* Lucinda at the side of the stage in her shorts was warming up.

Red looked up at Heather. "The legs are here," she mouthed.

Lucinda broke into the splits . . .

The postman dropped a pole.

"Oops, sorry," he shouted.

"Quiet," shouted Derek.

Agnus, finishing her line, attempted an unscripted comic *ta-da* tap dance.

"No tap dancing," said Derek.

A glockenspiel twinkled.

"And no glockenspiels . . ."

Heather watched as Lucinda moved to her pole. She fingered the lever . . .

Not so invisible now, am I?

Heather had spent the afternoon with Red. Together, over two teas and a hot soya chocolate, Heather and Red took turns listening.

Red told her about the smoking incident the night before and Heather, tucking into her hot chocolate, waited until she was finished . . .

"He couldn't wait to get out of the house," said Red. "Didn't even stop for tea, even refused a beer. My father said it was the kiss that upset Toby, that I jumped too soon."

"A peck is hardly a jump," said Heather. "A shag is a jump, having breakfast the next day is a jump, but a goodbye peck?" She sighed. *What I wouldn't give for one of those . . .*

"Toby doesn't see it as a peck though," said Red. "And Helmut is dead against smoking."

"My hubby smoked for years," Heather muttered. "Didn't bother me."

"That's not really helping," said Red.

Heather drained her mug. "Loved the smell."

"Yes, but you're not a vegan or a greenie, are you," muttered Red.

"I'm drinking soya," said Heather, "and I recycle."

"Everyone recycles these days," muttered Red.

Heather pushed her mug aside and was about to enter into a spiel about Lucinda's way-too-tight hot pants when Red began to talk about Helmut's manifestation theory. How picturing what you wanted made it happen . . .

"Do you think I should visualise more?" said Red.

"Visualise?" said Heather.

"Yes, my son's not talking," said Red, "and Helmut hasn't answered my text . . ."

Heather didn't answer. She was visualising—a broken pole, a broken lever, with Lucinda standing at the bottom of the pole with nowhere to go. She pictured the audience waiting—moaning—jeering. She drank in the moment, Lucinda's discomfort with a catcalling crowd . . .

Then she felt rotten.

"This visualising bit, like voodoo without the doll," muttered Heather. "Don't you think?"

"Voodoo?" said Red. "There are no pins."

"Yes, but the making things happen," said Heather. "You could do some harm."

"We are not killing people," said Red. "Visualisation is a happy thing."

Heather stared down at the stage. She knew what would make her happy.

That night, while Heather stared down at the rehearsal from hell, Helmut in the laundry room pondered his love life. He sat inches from the tumble dryer, staring at it like it was a TV, his thoughts whirling like his sheets, until Gary breezed in.

Gary, clutching a basket of laundry, stared at the dried hen poop on the only spare chair.

"Jeez," he tutted. "More of the friggin' stuff."

Helmut didn't hear.

"So much for George's fencing," said Gary.

Helmut looked up, caught Gary flicking the poop, and almost smiled.

Gary wiped his hands. "May as well leave the gate open."

Helmut nodded.

"Chuck bread about the place."

Helmut continued to nod.

"And as for Charlie, he's too loved up to do anything. Anyone would think it was his first time." Gary laughed. "Love to know who controls the TV remote in that partnership."

"I am not a TV person," said Helmut.

"Did you hear it last night?" said Gary, shoving clothes into a machine.

"I had my headphones on," said Helmut.

"Rocking like the Rolling Stones . . . no moss growing there." Gary laughed.

"Maybe you should try some headphones," muttered Helmut.

Gary slammed the machine shut.

"Headphones? The wife would love that, already says I don't listen," said Gary. He watched Helmut pull sheets from the tumble dryer. "What's eating you, sunshine?"

Helmut, with a despondent sigh, began to fold his sheets. Gary, a man with a fondness for his fellow man, took an end and nodded to Helmut to fold.

Helmut began to talk of the smoking incident.

"Hmmm, the smoking vegan thing, I get it," said Gary.

"I had my suspicions . . ." muttered Helmut.

"The coughing, the smell—dead giveaway," said Gary.

". . . and to be honest," continued Helmut, "I was impressed."

Gary stopped. "What?"

"She was trying to give up," said Helmut.

"Give up?" said Gary. "A smoker giving up smoking is like a German giving up his sausage." He chuckled.

Helmut stared out the window, oblivious to Gary's laughter, and sighed.

"It's the son. I thought we were friends, going to save the world together." He turned to Gary. "Are all teenagers so . . ."

"Dramatic?" said Gary.

". . . black-and-white?" said Helmut.

"Well, yeah," said Gary, "especially when the mother fancies another man . . . and is prepared to give up the fags for him."

Gary patted the folded sheet into the basket as Helmut pulled another from the dryer.

Gary continued, "I mean she didn't give up the smokes for Toby, did she? But she did for you."

"Mothers and sons," muttered Helmut.

"He must be spewing, and no amount of tofu is going to ease that pain . . ."

"Spewing?" muttered Helmut.

"Yes, like pissed?" said Gary. He slid a comrade arm around Helmut's shoulder. "My wife was always putty in her son's hands."

"Oh?" said Helmut.

"But he grew up, moved out, teenagers always do," said Gary sagely. He looked at Helmut. "So will Toby."

Helmut smiled with relief, and Gary was just on the verge of offering him a beer when George ran in with a panicked look . . .

"Two hens are missing."

The two men looked up.

"Last seen heading for Tesco's," said George.

"Tesco's?" said Gary.

Helmut stopped. "The roundabout . . . the lorries!"

"One was running like the clappers," said George.

"Clappers?" said Helmut.

"Fast," Gary said to Helmut.

"The postman's cornered Jess," said George. "With a roll and sausage."

"Nothing outruns a hen," muttered Helmut.

"Or beats a sausage," said Gary.

That night, Heather finished early and headed home. She passed the sound desk and with wave asked the girls to "mind and switch off the lights."

Ella nodded as Alisa packed the instruments away in a temper.

"That Lucinda thinks she's it," said Alisa, ramming her cymbals into their case. "My mum says she's asking for it."

Ella stopped. "For what?"

Alisa snapped the case shut. "She didn't say."

"You haven't been moaning to her, have you?" said Ella.

"Just about the friggin' wind machine and Miss Perfect's timing," said Alisa. "I mean it's not me that's wrong, it's her and her stupid pole dancing." Alisa crashed the cymbals case onto the floor. "And she's not *that* good."

"And you said this to your mother?" said Ella.

Alisa nodded.

"Jesus," muttered Ella.

Neither saw Lucinda standing behind them.

Chapter Fourteen

THE DRESSING-DOWN

Life Is Never the Same Once You Catch Your Mother Out.

By the time Alisa's mother arrived to pick up Alisa and Ella, Lucinda was giving Alisa a dressing-down, and Alisa was rising to the occasion like a politician on news night while her pal was doing her best to be invisible.

"The sound effects are meant to fit in with *my* pole dancing and not the other way around," said Lucinda.

"It's only a five-minute dance, hardly that important," said Alisa.

Ella quietly slid her glockenspiel sticks into their case.

"Well the postman says those five minutes are pivotal," snapped Lucinda.

"And he would know, wouldn't he?" said Alisa.

"As a matter of a fact he does," said Lucinda. "And he says you need to time your wind sound with the wind machine, or else . . ."

"Or else what?" said Alisa.

"I will look like an idiot," snapped Lucinda.

Alisa eyed Lucinda in her skintight rehearsal hot pants clutching a co-op bag. "I think you manage to that all by yourself," she said and turned to her bosom buddy. "Doesn't she?"

Ella, clicking the glockenspiel case shut, said nothing.

Lucinda called Alisa a "jumped-up twerp" and was moving on to more personal insults when Alisa's mother walked in—a formidable woman who had teachers cringing, shopkeepers running for cover, and the parking ticket person tearing up tickets.

The only person she didn't frighten was her daughter.

"Who are you to speak to my Alisa like that?" said Alisa's mother.

"Mother, I can speak for myself," said Alisa.

"Honestly, she has better things to do than orchestrate your wind," said Alisa's mother.

"Mum, there's no need for you to get involved," said Alisa.

"Anyone can orchestrate wind," snapped Lucinda.

"Exactly," said Alisa's mother.

"My point too," said Lucinda.

Derek arrived to smooth things over as Alisa and Ella, under Alisa's mother's "leave this to me" order, slipped into the car, embarrassed beyond embarrassment.

"Jesus, my mother is the pits," said Alisa.

Ella threw her a "poor you" comrade look.

"I had her, another few minutes and she'd be bawling," said Alisa.

"Bawling? I don't think so," muttered Ella. "Another few minutes and we'd be out of the panto, Lucinda's *like that* with the rest of 'em."

Alisa eyed Ella's crossed-finger gesture with a tut.

"She's the one pulling in the crowd," muttered Ella, "not our glockenspiel."

"Aye right," huffed Alisa, who was about to launch into a lecture about how indispensable they were to the panto production when her mother slid into the car.

"Well that's that sorted," she snapped.

"Sorted? What do you mean?" said Alisa.

"That shorts-wearing floozie will never talk to you like that again," said the mother.

"That shorts-wearing floozie has a name," snapped Alisa.

"Name? Who cares? I told them you're not going back in there, and"—she nodded to Ella—"neither should you." Alisa's mother switched on the engine and, with a rev, caught Ella's eye in the rear vision mirror. "Not if you want to see my front door again."

"Thanks," muttered Alisa, staring out the window. "I can rely on you to ruin everything."

Heather left the panto rehearsal and took a detour to Tesco's. Soon she was caught in a traffic jam; apparently two hens were on the loose. She sighed; all she wanted was some butter for her morning toast and here she was stuck at the roundabout, in Lochgilphead. *Who'd have thought it?*

The postman ran by clutching a hen with half a roll in its mouth. He saw Heather and waved with one of his annoying jaunty grins. The postman, it seemed, enjoys being a hero, even with a hen.

Typical, thought Heather.

A van tooted.

Another driver told him to "shut it."

Heather watched as Helmut charged past, followed by Gary and George. In the distance, she saw another hen fluttering above the bonnet of a blue delivery van, followed by a squawk from Helmut.

Red tapped on the passenger's window of Heather's car. "It's a hen," she said, laughing, "running around like it's headless—*in* Lochgilphead."

Heather stretched across and with a smile unwound the window.

"Just came in for some chewing gum," said Red. "Last thing you expect to see is a hen giving those bozos a run for their money."

Heather nodded. "I know." Then she pulled a face as the postman approached. He tapped on her window. She, with a grunt, unwound it.

"Be a luv" he said.

"What?"

"Hold the hen."

Heather threw a look a Red.

"The poor thing's distressed," said the postman.

"Lucinda's not around to help you?" snapped Heather.

The postman, thinking Heather was joking, laughed. "Her? She hates animals. Can't see her with a hen under her arm. Can you?"

Toby sat in his mother's car watching the hen duck and dive about the petrol pumps as the staff, along with various other people, ran about like morons. The hen looked like it was having a high old time, but Toby knew different. He knew it was scared . . .

The hen fluttered past Red's car and was about to settle on the boot when it recognised that funny fella that crept by the caravan steps. The hen stopped, blinked, then made for the only safe place it could see: Helmut's shoulder.

Helmut was about to squeal when he caught sight of Toby sitting in the passenger seat of Red's car and Red watching from Heather's car . . .

He froze. *Shit.*

The hen nestled into the side of his head, clucking. Helmut could feel the feathers ruffle against his neck; he could smell the grassiness of the bird as she clawed his shoulders, searching for balance. Helmut's stomach turned—his heart pounded as his knees began to twitch.

"Good man," shouted Gary.

Helmut said nothing.

"Stay still," shouted the postman from his van.

Toby's face softened.

Red slid back in the car. "I thought he hated birds—had a phobia," said Red.

"He does," said Toby. He opened the door. "There's a good girl," he whispered.

The hen blinked and dug her claws in, and hot poop dribbled onto Helmut's shirt.

Shit . . .

"Jump in," muttered Toby.

The postman reversed the van into the caravan park. Heather jumped out of the other side, her arms wrapped about the hen.

She slid the hen over the fence and watched it flap across to the pond. She tried to hide her pleasure, just as she had in the van.

The postman, however, wasn't fooled. He saw her cooing quietly in the revision mirror.

"She's a beaut, isn't she?" he said. "Wouldn't mind a few myself."

Heather watched the hen make itself at home about the water.

She took in a deep breath and tried to enjoy the moment—not think of going home and the panicky feeling that would take over . . .

Every morning she woke to an overwhelming feeling of dread, tears in her eyes, and a pointless future. She poured coffee, switched things on and off, and tried to console herself; nothing helped. The empty house was killing her.

Occasionally she tried to speak to someone, but always the words dried up. In fact, the only time she was verbal was with the postman. He and his annoying habits pushed her like no one else did. There was no time for panic attacks when he was around. There was too much to do—climbing ladders, holding screws—and he just assumed . . .

She turned to see the postman return from the van swinging a hammer by his side.

How annoying can one man be?

"Just quickly sort that fence." He handed Heather his nail bag. "Can you hold these?"

"You think I got nothing better to do?" she said.

"Only take a few minutes," said the postman.

"You always say that," huffed Heather.

"Should have asked me in the first place," muttered the postman. "This fence is an abortion of a job."

You always say that too, thought Heather with a small smile.

Chapter Fifteen

THE LAUNDRY ROOM

If You Repeat Something Often Enough, You Believe It.

*H*elmut sat in the laundry room staring at his shirt swirling in the washing machine. He had spent what seemed like hours (ten minutes) frozen in the back of Red's car with a hen digging into his shoulders and Toby commanding him to stay still. Ten minutes of a hen pooping like its life depended on it and Toby lecturing him with his "the hen's more frightened than you" theory . . .

Helmut wanted to shout, "Shut the Kroonenberg up, *you* try and sit still while claws dig into your skin, hot poop burning through your only clean shirt."

But he didn't. The last thing he wanted to do was cause any more hen flapping . . . instead he seethed.

Charlie handed Helmut a coffee while Toby talked of the psyche of a hen to Gary.

"The thing to remember," said Toby, "is that they are more frightened than you. Most birds are, except of course for birds of prey."

Helmut, wiping his neck with a wet wipe, turned to Gary. "I thought you said you'd stopped feeding hens that takeaway puke."

"Takeaway puke," said Gary, "takes a while to work through the system."

"And it's all organic," chipped in Toby.

"Organic?" Helmut snapped, glaring at Toby. "Most shit is. Still doesn't mean it's OK to have it spewing down your back like . . . like . . . spew."

"Only said," muttered Toby.

That afternoon, Toby, muttering his "the bird's more frightened than you" lecture, held tools for Heather and the postman as they mended the fence . . .

Neither listened.

Heather was busy waiting for an excuse to tut at the postman, while the postman was pulling at the escape hole—which, to quote him, was "big enough for an elephant."

Heather told him not to exaggerate.

Toby was confused and hurt. He had tried to help Helmut—he didn't have to, but he did out of the goodness of his heart—and what did he get for his time? A sermon about "friggin' spew and poo."

German knob.

Toby threw a stone into the pond and watched it plop. "Hens are just birds." He muttered, "Only an idiot is frightened of a bird."

The postman stopped and looked at Toby. "What's eating you?"

"Leave the boy alone," said Heather.

"You look like you've lost a pound and found a penny," said the postman.

"That's a stupid saying," said Heather.

Toby tossed another stone. "I'm fed up."

"What you got to be fed up about?" said the postman. "A young man like you, the whole world in front of you. You're smart, intelligent, you can do anything you want . . . in fact, we could do with you at the pan-to."

Toby looked at him. "Me?"

"Yes, the sound effect girls haven't a clue," said the postman.

"They are idiots," muttered Toby.

The postman jumped over the fence onto the pond side and bent to investigate the escape hole. A few of the hens clucked about his squatted figure.

The postman eyed Toby. "A smart young man like you could swing the whole chase scene around."

"Chase scene?" said Toby.

"What's wrong with the chase scene?" said Heather.

"Timing," muttered the postman.

"Timing?" snapped Heather. "There's nothing wrong with the timing."

No one saw the drake loitering under a bush, large and angry. A drake that had been removed from a farm full of happy hens, ducks, and excellent scraps. A drake now fenced in, cut off from his supply of scraps around the caravan. A drake who didn't recognise the noisy stranger with no bucket of food, no cooing sound . . . just a bum with something shiny peeking from it.

The drake focused on a nail poking through the postman's back pocket, his bill posed like a torpedo . . .

"If the timing's not right, the pole dancing goes out the window," said the postman.

Toby stopped mid stone toss. *Pole dancing?*

The postman stood up, then shifted uncomfortably. "Besides, just bumped into Charlie—the sound effect girls have walked out."

"I knew it," said Heather. "You just had to nag, didn't you, you and your bleeding timing."

"Mum never said anything about a pole dancer," muttered Toby.

Helmut stared out the laundry window. He had just heard about the sound team from Charlie, who, knowing Helmut was "in radio," asked for his help.

Helmut jumped at the chance to see Red with no Toby around. Fantastic . . .

All he had to do was press a few buttons while watching Red on stage. Then they could talk, have coffee, he could even walk her home.

His heart raced at the thought . . .

The drake was fast, like lightning, and no one saw him until he hit his target.

The postman jumped.

He turned to see the drake hissing through a gaping hole large enough to accommodate a football.

"Jesus!" he yelled as he pole-vaulted over the fence.

Helmut watched from the laundry room as the surprisingly agile postman scaled the fence like a prized Olympian.

"Impressive," he muttered.

"Olympic," said Gary.

"Almost pantomime," said Charlie.

The postman landed on the other side of the fence to a silent audience.

Regaining his balance, he snapped, "What bastard put that thing in there?"

Toby, about to launch into his "they're more afraid than you" sermon, caught sight of the drake and changed his mind. The drake had the wingspan of a two-man tent, and the last thing it looked was frightened.

Heather watched the postman dusting himself off and began to talk of swans that broke arms with their wings, until Toby pointed out it was not a swan.

"Timing," she muttered. "It's all about timing."

And for the first time ever, the postman glowered at her.

Chapter Sixteen

MORONS

One Man's Moron Is Another Man's Saint.

The next day, Helmut trotted down his skid-free steps. There was not a poop in sight. He stood at the bottom and stared at the superbly fenced-in pond. He wanted to thank the postman almost as much as he wanted to see Red again.

A hen peered through the fence and squawked at him.

It seemed like a hello, like she was missing the steps, its shelter, and Gary's Indian leftovers.

The hen blinked at Helmut.

He looked at his toast oozing with peanut butter.

"There you go . . ." he muttered and tossed it at her.

The other hens fluttered around followed by the drake.

Helmut stopped, thought, went back inside, and brought out his bucket of vegan scraps.

He emptied it over the fence and watched as the hens tucked in along with the drake. He thought about the hen on his shoulders, her warm body, and the vibrating of her clucking.

She didn't hurt him . . . she didn't even peck.

He pushed a finger through the fence, touched a feather.

It wasn't that bad . . .

That night he brought more scraps, and the next morning, as he opened the caravan door, the hens were there at the fence clucking with anticipation. He ventured near the gate, and the hens went mental, greeting him with waggling tails; the drake without a hiss was not far behind.

Helmut loved the greeting, as much he loved that his waste finally had a home.

An emergency technical rehearsal was organised to acclimatize the new sound team. There was no cast, just Toby, Heather, the postman, Charlie, Derek, and Helmut.

Toby arrived early, ready to save the day; he had no idea he had a partner. Neither did Helmut.

Helmut walked in, saw Toby engrossed in the script, and stopped. Toby flashed a look back, then reverted to his script, pretending to read.

Helmut, covering his surprise, pulled up a seat beside him and coughed.

Neither said anything.

The evening was busy, too busy for Helmut and Toby to mind each other. Instead they had to work together . . . which they did in speechless fashion with the odd nod.

It wasn't easy, but thanks to Heather and the postman's constant yelling at each other, Toby and Helmut had something apart from each other to focus on.

There was lots of plugging into sockets, dragging leads across the floor, and the postman yelling . . .

"No, not that one."

"Bring it here."

"Can you try that switch again?"

. . . while Heather told the pair to "just ignore the ignoramus," before following the said ignoramus's advice herself.

In the end, the chase scene was a quick walk-through with emphasis on the pole cover drop which, according to the postman, was as *pivotal as the wind machine.*

Heather, on a beam above, shouted, "If I hear that *P* word one more time, I am going to ram that pole in a very uncomfortable place."

Helmut laughed like a hyena, while Toby sighed.

The postman, oblivious to all ramming of poles, shouted, "Pull the lever quickly—timing is pivotal."

Heather, in a temper, crunched the lever.

The cover dropped to the floor in a flash . . .

The postman pulled it back to its covering position.

"Try it again," he shouted, "and not so fast this time."

She eased the lever slowly . . .

"Faster than that, we ain't got all day," shouted the postman.

"Will you make up your friggin' mind," shouted Heather.

Toby, in position by the wind machine, waited for the nod, which he missed three times until Helmut took over.

Finally, frazzled Toby arrived home to find his mother lounging in front of the TV and laughing with Kim.

Typical, thought Toby. *They're laughing it up while my life is a pile of wank.*

"Have fun?" said Red.

"Hardly, working with knobs who call shouting at each other banter." He huffed. "Their idea of a joke is any comment about the friggin' pole and its cover."

"I hear there's a pole dancer," said Kim teasingly.

Toby blushed. "Not today," he said. "It was a technical rehearsal."

Red watched Toby retreat to his room with a door slam.

"I hear Helmut was there," yelled Red.

"He's a moron," Toby shouted through his door, "and thanks for telling me."

Red threw a look at Kim as Toby turned his music on full volume.

Chapter Seventeen

LUCINDA

Wondering What Is Beneath Is Erotic; Seeing It Is Sex.

Toby and Helmut arrived early for the dress rehearsal, held at the Heavenly Space retirement village. Toby and Helmut were given a corner the size of a phone box, which made touching inevitable. In silence they set up the sound desk, working in sync. Toby saw the looks between Red and Helmut and huffed.

He was standing by the sound desk, lining up his glockenspiel hammers and whistles for the first scene. He was feeling fed up with the whole working-beside-his-mother's-possible-boyfriend thing—the man who had brushed aside his help—and the last the thing he expected to see was *her*... looking as she did.

He had told his mother he wasn't helping the panto for the pole dancing. He had brushed off his sister's "Toby's in luuuuuv" teasing, and he'd almost believed himself—until he saw *her*, a woman as he had never imagined.

Lucinda strutted onto the makeshift stage in her skintight leggings and thigh-high boots, waking up every elderly man apart from the visually impaired.

Toby's glockenspiel crashed to the ground.

Helmut picked up the glockenspiel, and when Toby missed his queue, Helmut grabbed his hammer and took over.

In fact, Helmut took over whenever Lucinda entered the stage. One glimpse of Lucinda's thighs had Toby fumbling, dropping, and losing his timing; soon the postman was beginning to panic. He had everything synched, timed, and paired down to a second. Now, Toby's adolescent crush threatened the very essence of his work and all those months of preparation.

It could all go tits-up.

Catching Helmut's eye, the postman mimed, *What the hell is going on?*

He had given up trying to catch Toby's attention; Toby had that spaced-out look any teacher or parent would have recognised. He was on another planet: Planet Adolescence, where hormones pulsated through the veins, turning concentration to mush.

Heather tried to calm the postman with reassuring looks and "Helmut's coping" mimes. Once the first act had finished, she raced to the postman standing by the beverage table backstage. She stared at his flushed face. This was a new panicky postman she had never seen before.

"It's a lucky thing Helmut has a cool head," said the postman, spooning sugar into his coffee, "because Toby's has gone out the bloody window."

Heather watched his shaky hand stir as Helmut paused for a coffee.

The postman tugged at his arm. "Can you multitask?"

"'Multitask' is Helmut's middle name," said Heather. She looked at Helmut. "Isn't it?"

Helmut nodded an "of course."

"Because you'll need to make those two hands of yours work like four, think on your feet for two, and"—the postman sighed—"not upset the poor boy."

Helmut smiled. "Yes," he said, "we have all been there."

He thought of Red, peering from her hood with a quirky expression. She had a way with her lines, of skipping through the woods clutching her basket, and was, as far he was concerned, the only woman worth watching.

He wanted to give her the best sound effects ever.

"Your pantomime is safe," he said. "My hands do the work of an army, and my feet are quicker than a flash of the lightning."

That night, Red served free-range eggs, decaf, and a protein boast as Toby silently ate.

His sister teased him, yet again . . . she thought the whole pole dancing incident was hilarious. Toby thought it was the most painful moment of his life.

Toby had never noticed the opposite sex before, and when he saw Lucinda wrap her legs around the pole, his legs quivered. He had a prime position. The sort of position most men only dreamed of. A bird's-eye view of parts of a woman he had only heard of, covered in skintight silk leaving little to the imagination.

And that *little* worked overtime.

As her legs spread into a V shape, Toby, like a rabbit caught in headlights, was struck dumb. Hypnotised by the silk-covered crotch of Lochgilphead's most famous barmaid, Toby's knees buckled, and with a loud crash he stopped the wind machine as he went down.

"If it wasn't for Helmut, you'd be up the creek without a paddle," laughed Kim. "Or in your case a pole."

"I'm not in it for the pole dancing," Toby lied and stomped to his room.

Toby's infatuation with Lucinda caused him great pain, and Heather rose to the occasion. She suggested a better place for the wind machine and worked with Helmut to reduce Toby's work to a minimum. But nothing eased his pain, and over the next week, as the pantomime cast performed for Lochgilphead and beyond, Toby froze, dropped things, and blushed redder than a tomato. His brain turned to marshmallow whenever Lucinda appeared on the stage, and he spent the rest of the time recovering, wishing he could find a duvet to hide under.

Toby's confidence plummeted while Helmut tactfully did everything, which for a man used to the demands of live radio was a doddle to him.

Heather, however, loved being backstage, scaling the beams, creating magic. She loved working under pressure—the audience, the applause, the laughter, watching the postman skirt about like his life depended on it.

And the timing, how she loved the timing . . . finally all the pivotal lectures made sense and she fell in love with the word, texting her daughter with backstage images and how pivotal each piece of equipment was.

Heather felt alive and she didn't want the show to end.

Each night was a new crisis and each morning Heather woke with a solution. She bounced out of bed, sprinted to the co-op for biscuits, and texted the postman.

"Let's try a timer for the strobe lights . . . ."

Or

"How would sandbags work around the wind machine . . ."

And the postman always replied, "Good thinking, Missus . . ."

On the final night, the calico cover refused to drop. Heather wrestled with the jammed lever, which finally, after the postman's "give it a good tug," propelled off in her hands and clanged down to the stage.

The audience laughed . . .

Heather froze. She looked down at Lucinda. The poor cow looked lost.

"Shit," mouthed the postman and made his way up the beam as the dame and fairy godmother improvised.

There wasn't much room on the beam.

"Budge up," whispered the postman. He inspected the remains of the lever.

Heather could feel the heat from the postman's body as he wrestled with the calico strings wedged into the remains of the lever.

It was stuck like glue.

"They have fused," he muttered, "from the heat of the lights." He looked into her eyes and his heart stopped.

"The wind machine," whispered Heather.

The postman's face lit up. He, with a wink at Heather, nodded to Helmut.

When the curtains closed on the final bow, Heather hid a tear.

The postman noticed, and with a gentle pat on her shoulder he said, "Come on, girl, we got packing to do before the aftershow party."

"Party," she muttered. "Who could party?"

The fun was over just as it got started.

"Lucinda wants to thank you," said the postman.

Heather blushed. "It was nothing."

"Nothing? You saved her from a fate worse than death: ad-libbing. Lucinda may have legs, but she can't think on her feet."

Heather shrugged; she couldn't help herself. When she saw Lucinda lost under the spotlight, she had to do something despite her friggin' hot pants. And when the dame and the fairy godmother began to ad-lib, it was easy. She just swivelled the spotlight off Lucinda and onto them.

Toby breathed a sigh of relief when the panto was over. As the cast bowed to the audience, Helmut and Red smiled at each other; Toby didn't notice, and when the spotlight flashed onto the sound desk, Toby, with a grimace, waved. All he could think about was retreating to his bedroom and returning to his "save the world" books.

The morning after the final panto performance, Helmut posted his latest blog and made his way to the pond.

Since the postman had high-jumped over the pond fence, few had ventured inside. George had a go; he bent to pick an egg, but his builder's crack—nice and tender—was too much for the drake. With one peck, George squealed "louder than a castrated pig" and vowed to become vegan, while Charlie decided to buy eggs from the co-op from then on.

Helmut felt for George and his pale backside and he wanted to help. He tipped his vegan waste over the fence and stared out onto the hens and drake pecking . . .

What would tame a drake?

He was just thinking about a trip to the library when a small ball of bread sailed past his ear and landed at the feet of a chick.

He turned to see Toby.

"You know anything about drakes?" said Helmut.

Toby's face softened. "Only that they mate for life."

❋

Heather answered her front door to see nothing but a potted miniature rose. She picked it up and read the attached note.

There are plans for a production for the drama festival. And they need
backstage hands. I can't do it without you.
The postman [Smiley face]

Heather slid her pot plant onto the windowsill and texted back.

As long as there are levers that need oiling, I'll be there.

She swithered over to the emojis, finally settling on a laughing face. Within seconds, the postman texted back

Fantastic
[Happy face]
[Laughing face]
[Kissing face]
[Two kisses]

Helmut and Toby headed off to a farm nearby that had geese. They watched the geese parade about the field as a young farmer approached.

"That's her," he said, pointing to a young goose. "She'd be perfect for your drake and you'll get eggs as well."

No one noticed as a young woman approached. Toby saw her first, and for once he didn't blush. Lucinda in a duffel coat, wellies, and ponytail looked more like one of his sister's pals than an exotic dancer.

A goose fluttered past her. She jumped, screeched, and slid her arm into the farmer's.

Toby laughed. "There's nothing to be afraid of—the thing to remember is that they are more afraid of you than you are of them."

"That's what he says," said Lucinda with nudge at the farmer. The farmer laughed as Lucinda pecked his cheek.

That night, Toby walked into the kitchen and saw his mother wrestling with a nut roast that refused to gel; the sides flopped apart.

"What's with the nut loaf?" he said.

"Helmut's coming around for tea," said Red.

"Oh?" He looked almost pleased.

"You OK with that?" said Red. "I thought we could celebrate the whole geese thing."

Toby plonked himself at the table next to his sister and laughed.

"Yes, let's see what that German knob has to say," he said as his sister answered the door.

***

Guess what there is more!

"Lockdown" the fourth book in the series. Would you like to hear what the drama group get up in Lockdown?

Turn the page for a taster or you can order at your favourite store.

Chapter One-In The Beginning

"Toilet brush" is no name for a hairdo.

George stood at the Red Cross shop counter eyeing the half price sticky-note on a TV. Behind it, staring from the pocket-size screen, was the PM.

George stared at his blond hair that looked way too much like a toilet brush.

"Thank God that's on mute."

No one heard. The shop was empty apart from two staff bent under the counter shoving mugs and packets of biscuits into a box like there was a food embargo.

George idly wondered what the full price for the TV was as he dumped two garbage bags onto the counter with a grunt. They were heavy, full of an unwanted pair of curtains, courtesy of Catrina.

She, waking up one too many times to the "abortion of a curtain," declared that either they go or she does.

He had to admit they were a bit drab. Seventies secondhand. In fact, they probably came from this very shop.

He watched the two staff, an elderly woman with a commanding chest and a bookish-looking young man with stiff hair. They were packing, completely oblivious to him and his bags.

He coughed and was on the verge of shouting a Brexit joke when the door crashed open.

The till drawer followed, spraying a fountain of coins onto the floor.

"Turn it up," said the voice.

"And listen to that twat?" muttered the elderly woman.

She looked up, caught sight of the face behind the voice, and smiled.

"Oh, it's you."

"The PM's on," said the postman. "We should listen. It's an update."

"We already know what the update is," said the elderly woman with a crisp shutting of the till.

"It all kicks off midnight," said the young man from under the counter.

"Kicks off?" said George.

"Lockdown," said the elderly woman with a heave of her chest. "You've five minutes. We're closing."

"What about my curtains?" said George.

She pushed the bags toward him. "Take 'em home."

"But . . ."

"I'm a volunteer. I'm not paid for sorting in the face of an epidemic; that's frontline work."

"You *have* had your flu jab, Gran," came the muffled voice of the young man.

"Flu jab? That's as useful as the shop's till *and* as out of date."

The door burst open again.

The till drawer followed, hurling a few remaining coins to the floor.

Catrina, dressed in her casual I'm-not-at-work-but-rather-hiking attire, filled the doorway. Her hair, usually up and rigid, looked wispy about the edges as her muscular arms clung to several garbage bags.

She glared at George with a "where the hell have you been?" look.

A garbage bag dropped; she didn't move.

"We're to take it back, luv," said George.

"What?" snapped Catrina.

"They're closing," said George.

"Things are kicking off," said the postman.

"You *are* kidding," snapped Catrina.

"No, I'm friggin' not. It's the Chinese," said Gran, slamming the till shut.

"And that twat," the postman said, gesturing to the TV. "We'll be wearing masks next."

"Over my dead body," said Gran. "We're not the Chinese; fresh air is good for you."

"But we've just had a clear-out," said Catrina.

"Them and their cats in cages," said Gran.

"It's bats," said the young man.

"Apparently they strangle them beside their special fried rice. They have no idea about health and safety."

Everyone looked at her.

"I *was* a chef, you know."

"Dinner lady, Gran."

"I do have a fair idea of hygiene, and those from the far *whatever* are about as clean as a dog's kennel. Stringing cats up outdoors . . ."

"It's bats!" said the young man.

"And all that blood." She shook her head.

"Where else would you string things up?" laughed the postman.

"Well, not near my fried rice, for a start," said Gran.

The young man thrust a Nescafé jar into a bag and stood up.

"Gran, you're getting silly again."

"Those Chinese have lived for thousands of years on bats," said the postman.

"Exactly," huffed Gran.

"And look at them—their old folk dance in the street, not like ours, shoved in front of a TV too comatose to dribble."

Gran huffed her chest, standing at attention. "I think you exagger-ate. I've yet to meet a dribbler in my circle of so-called old friends."

"Gran, have you taken your tablets?" said the young man.

"And what am I to do with these bags?" huffed Catrina in her crisp

German accent.

"We'll find something," muttered George.

"I'm not friggin' carting them back. I have better things to do with my attic."

"I said we'll sort it, luv."

"Attic. Well, that says it all," said Gran. "There'll be all manner of infections in that lot. Get them out of my shop."

"Tablets, Gran?"

"I have cleaned these on the hottest wash," said Catrina.

"Ninety degrees *ain't* gonna kill a Chinese virus."

George gestured to the car. "Let's go, pet."

Catrina huffed. "What am I to do with all this . . . stuff?"

"We could use *my* stuff for costumes," said George.

"Costumes?" said Catrina. "Out of these so-called curtains?"

George glared at her.

"I wouldn't hang them on a window, let alone an actor."

"I beg to differ, *luv*," hissed George.

Gran looked at George, "That's where I know you: the infamous fire."

George face stiffened. "That hall was buggered."

"Still, a hall," said Gran.

George stomped back to the car, stuffed the bags into the boot, and pressed the top down for all it was worth.

He was fed up with the fire.

Of all the things he had done in his life—the pantos he had directed, his famed *Dick Whittington*, his *Puss in Boots*, and his much-talked-about *Peter Pan*—none mattered but that bloody fire.

Catrina said nothing. When anyone mentioned the fire, it was best to leave him to "huff himself out," as she called it.

"They got a new hall out of it," he muttered, "but do they thank me?"

"Let's just get in the car," said Catrina.

George jumped into the driver's seat and revved the engine.

Catrina threw him an "easy on the peddle" look.

Gran stood at the shop door and switched the Open sign to Closed with a prophetic glare.

He huffed. "Wasn't that long ago that old witch was laughing her head off at my *Puss in Boots*."

Catrina, with her best soft look, patted his knee.

"My *Dick Whittington* was so innovative it made the center page."

The grandson appeared, tablet in hand. Gran ignored his nudges and continued to stare.

George, meeting her glare, revved his engine again. "But what does *she* remember?"

"Let's just head off," muttered Catrina.

"The friggin' fire."

"Let's not go there, dear."

"Granny's friggin' Soup Kitchen going up in flames."

"It *was* her Wendy house," said Catrina.

"I'll die with it plastered on my gravestone. 'Here lies George, the man who burnt good old Gran's friggin' Wendy house,'" he grumped. "And me their best customer."

"You want them to write *that* on your gravestone?"

"I've been in that shop more times than the cleaner. I practically paid their wages with the stuff I've brought over the years."

"They're volunteers," said Catrina.

"Well, the electric bill then." He stared ahead as the car hummed in neutral.

"Do you want me to drive?" snapped Catrina.

He crunched into first and headed off like a rally driver.

"Love to show her and her cronies."

"I'm sure we can do something," said Catrina.

"Make 'em eat their friggin' words."

Catrina stared at the road ahead. "Not much chance of that now, is there? We're in lockdown."

***

order at your favourite store

A NOTE FROM THE AUTHOR

I hope you enjoyed Helmut's adventures inspired by my time
performing in the local pantomime although there was no fella called
Helmut.
There was however plenty of teenagers including two of my own...
Mine are now grown ups but I still remember those teenage year.
If you would like to leave a review I would be tickled pink.

You can find me at
www.kerrienoor.com
And

 facebook.com/kerrienoorwriter

 twitter.com/kezzamac

 instagram.com/kerrienoor

ALSO BY KERRIE NOOR

Bellydancing and Beyond series :-

Book 1 :-Sheryl's Last Stand

Book 2:- The Downfall of a Bellydancer

Book 3:- Four Weddings and a Funeral

All three Bellydancing and Beyond books are now available on Audio (fantastic!)

Book 4:-Three Angry Women And A Baby

Book5:- The Real Story Of 'O"

Planet Hyman Series:-

Book 1:-Rebel Without a Clue

Book 2:- Rebel Without a Bra

Book 3:- Rebel Without a Crew

All three books are now available on Audio (even more fantastic!)

Prequel 1:- The Rise Of Manifesto The Great

Prequel 2:- The Downfall Of Manifesto The Great

Prequel 3:- The Legacy Of Manifesto The Great

Diva Diaries Series:-

Novella 1:-A Dame Called Derek

Novella 2:- Panto Boy

Novella 4:- Lockdown

And

If you liked Panto Girl

please leave a review.

My gratitude will hold no bounds

Regards and cheers

Kerrie Noor